THE FORGERY

First published by Charco Press 2022
Charco Press Ltd., Office 59, 44-46 Morningside Road,
Edinburgh EH10 4BF

ISBN: 9781913867157
e-book: 9781913867164

www.charcopress.com

Edited by Fionn Petch
Cover designed by Pablo Font
Typeset by Laura Jones
Proofread by Fiona Mackintosh

Ave Barrera

THE FORGERY

Translated by
Ellen Jones & Robin Myers

CHARCO PRESS

To my father

But since you are worth teaching, and able to understand,
I will show you how little it would take
to finish this piece.

Honoré de Balzac, *The Unknown Masterpiece*

PART ONE

PART ONE

My name is José Federico Burgos. I'm a painter. I make copies of Renaissance paintings and the occasional forgery. I'm sitting on the edge of the highest wall on the property. I'm going to jump. I'm going to do it any second now. The dawn cold numbs my legs as they dangle over the abyss. The streetlamps are starting to turn off as the sunlight peeps over my shoulder. Sunbeams cut through the haze lying over the hamlet. I hear a cockerel's cry, but it must be miles away. This yellow morning light might be the last thing I see.

Now that it's getting brighter, I look down and try to calculate, again, the consequences of my fall: the wall is about six metres high, but then there's another fifteen- or twenty-metre slope of scrub and stone. The branches should help break the fall, but there's always a chance I'll crack my head open on a rock and be left paralysed. Not that I have any alternative. Going back to that house would be worse than plunging to my death.

I shift my weight over the edge and my buttocks begin to slip. No going back now – I'd have to hang on with both hands and one of them is already broken, cradled against my heart, smashed to pieces. I jump, pushing hard away from the wall, and scream in mid-air. It's a short, dry scream, and it reaches me as if someone else had screamed it. My nerves stand like barbs, registering the details of each millionth of a second. I can't feel the wind, just a force sucking at me like a dark mouth; the gap between my body falling and what it falls away from, along with my stomach. Like when you go over a dip in the road at full speed. Then my feet hit the ground and my whole weight comes smashing down. I may not weigh much, but six metres are six metres, and gravity does its work. My legs spasm and an electric shock runs up my torso to my arms. My head snaps back, although not too hard. Then immediately, movement. I'm dragged down through the stones and branches, skidding head-long between hard clods and rocks. I can't keep track of the scrapes and blows and grazes. In the cloud of dust I'm raising, the distance feels much further than I'd calculated. An eternal expanse in which everything crunches and cracks and rolls and rips, but I can't be sure whether what's crunching and cracking are branches or my own bones and flesh. I feel a stab in my side, a twinge that could just as well have been a thorn or something piercing deep into an organ – who can say, the pain is the same. *Flesh or bone?* is the only thing I can think. Flesh or bone.

Finally, I come to a halt. My blood beats in my temples, in my hands. I'm conscious. Stunned, but conscious. *My hand!* I think with a start, as though anticipating a pain that then instantly erupts, my right arm twisted to one side like a piece of spaghetti. My whole body is spaghetti-soft.

I open my eyes, or it feels like I open my eyes, into the gradually dispersing cloud of dust. I'm very close to the edge of the road – surely someone will see me, someone who'll pick me up and take me to hospital, or call an ambulance. It's just a question of waiting. Waiting and managing the pain. Staying very still so the pain doesn't take over my thoughts. Then I really would be lost. It's odd, the pain isn't localised in my broken arm any more, nor in my scrapes; it's a dull throbbing that envelops me entirely. Like a speaker muffled by a cushion.

I hear the drag of footsteps along the ground, to one side of my head. I can't turn to look. A force like a hand is stopping me. From the footsteps, I deduce that there are two people, but all I manage to see is the toe of a shoe. It's a leather shoe, a very fine one, perfectly clean, not a single blade of grass clinging to it.

'You won't be able to play with those clubs here. You need a five-wood titanium head, so you can lift it with those flimsy little biceps of yours,' I hear the closer voice saying.

'I've ordered some Dunlops, but they haven't arrived yet. Once they get here I'll give you a run for your money, you'll see. It won't do you any good trying to measure the course with your architect's eye,' the other replies, with the harsh accent of an old-time rancher.

The man in the clean shoes crouches down beside me.

'Let's go. Leave him, he's alive,' says the man further off.

'Did you see him jump? I think he's one of ours.'

'What else is he gonna be, man. Come on, take your shot and have done with it.' I hear the click of a lighter, then smell tobacco.

'Hey, kid… Kid, can you hear me?' the man by my side insists. I catch a momentary glimpse of his face: his wide bald head, his curly eyebrows and impish eyes.

'Hang on in there, they're on their way. We can talk when you get back,' I hear him say. He gets up and walks off.

'Yeah, get some rest in the cemetery!' his companion says, and they both laugh heartily.

'Bet you anything I'll make the next hole in three, tops.'

'You serious? With your arthritis? I'd bet on Miracle that you can't.'

'That horse is past his prime. And you'd gone grey before he was even born…'

I hear the clean sound of a ball being putted. The voices grow distant. I struggle to turn over but can't manage it. What they're saying makes no sense, there's no golf club here or anything like it, it's a patch of wasteland by the side of the road and I'm in urgent need of someone's help, someone who can call an ambulance.

My head finally frees itself of the weight that had kept it from moving, but there's nobody there. I'm surrounded by spiny shrubs, dry earth. Below me, a few metres away, I can just about see the black strip of asphalt and the gutter alongside it. I hear the roar of a large engine. The pain stirs. It's a shot that shatters every nerve, a lightning bolt into an old tree. It doesn't even leave me time to scream. The pain immediately absorbs all my strength and I'm unable to endure it. It's about to annihilate me when something surges from within my own mind and sucks me into its tiniest corner. A dark, quiet box where time stands still.

1.

I woke up that day to the cooing of pigeons. It was three or four months ago, when I lived in the little studio I'd rented on the corner of 30th and Mina, toward the front of one of those buildings with small flats around a shared patio that were fashionable in the fifties and then quickly went to seed. Although the place left much to be desired, it was at least cheap, and had good lighting and its own bathroom. There were only two rooms, both with a view of the street. One of them served as my studio and I somehow managed to use the other for everything else. I slept on a shiny velvet sofa, my clothes balled up in a couple of boxes of Foca laundry detergent, and I had a few books and papers on the windowsill. On a table improvised from Corona crates sat the television and a hotplate where I heated water for my Nescafé and made rabbit-skin glue for sizing my canvases. I also had a cream-coloured mini fridge I'd cool some beers in once in a blue moon.

To one side of the studio was a wooden table, an easel I'd fashioned myself, a shelving unit full of supplies and a swivel chair I'd picked up in the Baratillo market for a decent price. Leaning against the wall were four or five canvases in various stages of completion.

There was a knock at the door. I don't know if it was the first attempt, or if they'd been knocking for a while and that was what had woken me. It was too early, probably around eight, and in those days I wasn't used to getting up until after ten. I sat up on the sofa and saw two silhouettes through the frosted glass: the first, short and round, had to be the landlady, Doña Gertrudis. The other was a tall man built like a wardrobe.

It was odd, I thought, that Doña Gertrudis should have come a day earlier than we'd agreed to collect the four months' rent I owed, and even odder that she should come accompanied by someone I assumed was her nephew. Doña Gertrudis always found an excuse to talk about the achievements of her Panchito, a screwchewing hero who worked at the wholesale market and who, she claimed, could make the 12 December pilgrimage to Zapopan on his knees or carry a tank of gas on each shoulder without even breaking a sweat. I decided to keep quiet until they'd gone. They knocked again.

I realised I needed to go to the toilet. As I got up, I heard them insert a key into the lock. I froze, alarmed. Fortunately, I'd double-locked it the night before, so the man was jiggling the key in vain. I let out a silent laugh to shake off my irritation at the liberties they were taking. They murmured something and knocked again, this time so hard they must have chipped the paint. I waited until I was sure they'd gone before flushing the toilet. After splashing water on my face, I felt my fright and indignation subside and give way to anxiety. I was about to hit a new low in what had already been a bad spell, and I couldn't muster up the energy to haul myself out of it. I dug around in the box of clothes for a short-sleeved checked shirt and pair of jeans that wasn't too dirty, though they were all invariably stained with paint. It was too hot to put a vest on underneath.

In a corner of the studio leaned the Victorian triptych Señora Chang had commissioned me to restore. As much as I'd insisted I no longer did restorations, I was eventually won over by her bourgeois charm, her readiness to write a cheque and the fact I could no longer put off paying the rent. I gently touched the surface of the open side panels to see if the glaze I'd applied the night before was dry. It was still soft, but I was out of time, so I closed them over the central panel.

One of the disadvantages of waking up early, as anyone who has ever been poor will know, is hunger. In the fridge there was nothing but a shrivelled lemon in the egg tray and a rusted tin of chipotle chillies. I found half a packet of salted crackers among the tubes of paint. Once I'd checked it for bugs, I shoved the packet between my teeth, grabbed my keys, and carried the triptych out into the street. As soon as I closed the door I saw Doña Gertrudis and her grunt waiting for me next to my truck. I wavered for a moment, but there was nothing for it but to confront them. I started by dropping the packet of crackers so I could say good morning. Doña Gertrudis crossed her arms and lowered her gaze.

Her nephew swaggered forward: 'We were knocking for ages, why didn't you open up?'

'Yeah, I heard you, but I was in the bathroom and when I came out there was no one there. I also heard you trying to get in. You may not be aware that it's illegal to invade your tenants' privacy.'

For a moment the young bruiser seemed mildly intimidated, and I took the chance to address the landlady.

'What can I do for you, Doña Gertrudis?'

'Oh, I just wanted to see if you're able to pay those months you owe,' she replied in embarrassment, lowering her face and pulling her cardigan over her voluminous breasts.

The triptych was very heavy and I had no choice but to put it down, resting it on top of my foot.

'That's right, we agreed that tomorrow I'll settle the debt. I've no reason to go back on my word. As you can see, I'm on my way to deliver this piece of work and then I'll pay my dues. There's no need for you to try and break into my home, and certainly no need for a bodyguard.'

The guy went on the defensive, this time more angrily. 'In case you didn't know, I'm Doña Gertrudis's nephew, and from now on if you've any complaints you'll bring them to me, got it?'

'Of course, no problem. I'll square things tomorrow as we agreed, Doña Gertrudis.' I tried to head off to open the truck, but the thug got in my way.

'Nope, not tomorrow, no can do. You have twenty-four hours, you hear me?'

As clearly as I'd heard the line in a dozen films.

'Yeesh, you sure it can't be tomorrow?' I asked, panting with the effort of lifting the triptych into the back of the truck.

'Twenty-four hours,' he said again, his index finger in my face, 'or we'll dump all your crap in the street and you're out of here.'

'Fine, twenty-four hours it is. I promise I'll pay, Doña Gertrudis, don't worry. See you tomorrow, have a lovely day, OK?' I smiled as I started the engine and even waved goodbye.

As I drove through the streets of Country Gardens towards Señora Chang's house, I felt my confidence and aplomb gradually return.

Inside my truck, an almost new red '87 Chevrolet with only three years of use, I could feel in control of things. What will be will be – after all, if they turned me out I could always sleep in the truck, or just take off and go wherever I fancied. For the time being I had a quarter of a tank of petrol, enough for the rounds I had to do that day. In any case, I was going to have to get out of that apartment quickly and rent something better, some place where at least I didn't have to share space with such boorish people.

I arrived, rang the doorbell, and a familiar voice answered on the intercom.

'Morning, Mari. I'm here with the goods for Señora Chang.'

'I'm sorry, mister, she's not in right now. She might be back this afternoon, but I can't know for sure. She's away in Ajijic, on business.'

'Agh, you're kidding. How about I leave the delivery here and come back in the afternoon to see if she's home?'

'I can't do that, I'm afraid, Señora Chang won't like it. It'd be better if you try her a bit later.'

Cursing to myself, I lifted the triptych back into the truck and drove aimlessly around the neighbourhood. I didn't know what to do. The truth was, I had nowhere to go, and there was no point wasting what little petrol I had left, so I pulled over in a patch of shade next to a park. I reached for the packet of crackers and started eating, imagining what other people would be having for breakfast in this part of town: chilaquiles with chicken, sincronizadas with salami and Gouda cheese, cappuccinos. I cursed myself for having let things get this bad.

Since leaving Mendoza's studio I'd failed to achieve any kind of stability, and was feeling burned out. At first, I'd actually been excited by the idea of leaving behind that dull routine, painting countless copies of the same ubiquitous works people always bought: Mona Lisas, Bacchuses, Last Suppers. Since I started out on my own, I'd been painting less popular Renaissance works, ones I found even more impressive than the really famous ones. I was convinced people would appreciate the beauty of those paintings and become more open to different perspectives, slowly broadening the range of what they understood by art and discovering more interesting and original pieces to hang in their living rooms. In the medium term, once I'd built up some savings and a handful of established clients, I could start working as an artist in my own right. The plan demanded a great deal of effort, sure, but it had seemed worthwhile. I still don't understand how it failed so spectacularly.

I spent what little cash I had at the time on materials to paint a few canvases that I lugged back and forth from one gallery to another, from the Glorieta Chapalita outdoor exhibition space to the Trocadero on Avenida México. And it wasn't like my Titians and Vermeers were second-rate knock-offs. On the contrary: everybody stopped to look at them, ask me about them, check their prices. Gallery managers congratulated me on bringing something new to such a hermetic and conservative market. What hypocrites. When it came down to it, nobody was willing to pay what the pieces were worth and I had to sell them off cheap so I could clear the debts I'd run up, handing them round galleries like free samples of a new shampoo.

Slowly but surely, I lost heart. Painting didn't make any sense, but nor did doing anything else. I wasn't sure which of the two options was worse and I didn't want to decide. I didn't want to do anything. Didn't want to go back to doing traditional copies, didn't want to look for other work as a waiter or giving drawing classes in some college or workshop for amateurs. As a copyist, no matter how good I might be, I would always be buried under the weight of a five-hundred-year-old corpse; but as an artist I didn't have the contacts to get my name out there, nor the guts to survive the circling vultures who ran the provincial, hostile fiefdom that was Guadalajara.

My mouth was dry. I got out of the truck and walked into the park, where I was lucky enough to find a leaky tap. A puddle had formed around it and half a dozen black rooks were drinking there, though they bounced off as soon as they saw me. I brought my mouth to the tap to drink, then rinsed my face and neck. There was nothing to do except wait for Señora Chang, so I lay down on a bit of dry grass with my hands behind my head and fell into a deep sleep.

I woke up around midday, even more worried, suddenly convinced I shouldn't put all my eggs in one basket. I couldn't rely on Señora Chang's payment alone. What would happen if she didn't come back that afternoon? Or if she gave me a post-dated cheque, as she often did? 'Forgive me, José,' she'd said once, 'but I swear my husband wants to starve me to death. He's always complaining I spend too much, can you believe that? I went right out and told him he should leave politics and devote himself to faking banknotes.' Women with airs like that are so exasperating, I don't know why I always end up complying with their whims. One time I went over to paint a glass chandelier blue, and another time I even forged the name inscribed on a portrait of a countess, which I'm sure helped her argue her case in some family dispute.

No, Señora Chang and her ilk didn't have worries like mine. It occurred to me that I could visit Luckless Lalo, a rag-and-bone man on Avenida México who I knew from way back. He had bailed me out once and let me return the favour in kind, though he wasn't generally a charitable soul. He always found a way of coming out on top.

His real name was Lalo Salgado, but he was such a poor salesman that his fellow junk dealers had christened him Luckless Lalo. No matter how fine his merchandise was, it'd inevitably be stuck there for years, gathering dust among the mountains of other rubbish that refused to budge from his thrift shop – if it can even be called a shop, that windowless box with its metal shutters half-open to the street, where not even the flies stopped to look in.

I recognised the smell of dust and old sweat as soon as I arrived. Everything looked exactly as it had on my last visit. The desk stacked with old papers by the entrance, a fake leather chair with its ripped seams oozing spongy filling – occupied by Don Lalo's old, dirty white cat, her ear marred by a crescent-shaped bite, who lifted her head to acknowledge my presence before going back to sleep. From the back of the shop came voices and the clamour of a cantina.

I crossed the archipelago of furniture and dusty objects and peered in. As expected, there was the group of bohemian artists who regularly whiled away their afternoons at the shop, playing cards and talking politics and making their way through gallons of cheap Tonayan tequila watered down with soda or tap water. I knew them well. They were older than me, but they'd been around, on and off, forever – we shared favourite venues, parties, friends. They seemed to be omnipresent in their aimlessness. I usually tried to avoid them because I was terrified of becoming one of them, though I'd been heading steadily in their direction of late.

'Well look what the cat dragged in! How's it going, man?' Don Lalo's voice rang out, although he didn't get up or tear his gaze away from the poker hand in front of him. 'Sit down and get yourself a drink. Just let me finish polishing off this rookie.'

I leant against a cabinet and waved at the rest of the players: Juárez, the poet, with the usual dirty flower in his lapel; his girlfriend, a black widow who'd always wanted to be an actor and wore bright red, badly applied lipstick; a musician who sang ballads outside tourist bars in exchange for tips, and Spike, a pot-bellied punk who sold vinyl records with Roxie, and who believed his greatest achievement was having once eaten a whole, unsliced, family-sized pizza, rolled up like a taco.

Malinche, a sad, ageing hippie I'd briefly dated, offered me a glass of tequila and grapefruit soda. The drink was so warm it was almost hot, but the sweetness quenched my thirst and I downed it in a couple of swigs. The tequila tickled my empty stomach and I immediately felt the joints between my bones relax.

When the game was over, Don Lalo gave his seat to Malinche.

'Good to see you,' Don Lalo said, taking me aside, towards the shop. 'You really fell off the map this time, what happened?'

'I'm working on a big project,' I lied.

'For the museum?'

'No, all that dried up. It's a private client. Only I've run out of materials. I wanted to ask if you could lend me the money for them, and I'll get you back as soon as they pay me.' I was making the whole story up on the spot, without even thinking about it.

'Mmh, I'm in the same fix,' he said automatically.

'It would be a month at most.'

'I can't, mate, things are tough here. I've only just paid off some debts.'

We both knew we were lying. For one thing, I knew the money belt Lalo had hanging below his belly was always full of bills. I also knew his money came from some murky business that had nothing to do with the thrift shop.

'Fine, forget I said anything,' I said, a little annoyed, and headed for the door.

'Hang on, hang on. You remember the painting you left me that one time?'

'Titian's *Flora*?' I asked, searching it out among the mountain of objects.

'A customer bought it a couple of weeks ago. He was dying to talk to you, but I don't have your number. Why don't you call him, maybe he wants to commission something?'

'I don't know if I can,' I said, so as not to lose face. 'I'm neck deep in this other project, I'd have to finish that first.'

'Just talk to him, then at least he can tell you what it's about.'

Before I could invent another excuse, Don Lalo had the phone in his hand and was dialling the man's number.

'I'll call him later,' I tried to interrupt.

'Oh come off it, what's wrong with now. Hello? Señor Romero? Yes, that's right. I'm here with the painter… You know, the one who did the copy you bought.'

I swore quietly at Lalo, who was holding the handset out to me.

'Good afternoon, José Burgos speaking.' I made myself sound all serious.

'I need you to come. Can you stop by my office right now? I have an urgent job for you. It's very important.'

'Right now?' I stammered.

'Yes, it's extremely urgent. I'll wait here for you until 2 p.m. The office is on the corner of Américas and Joaquín Angulo, on the right-hand side; there's a big wooden gate. Ring the bell and ask for Horacio Romero.' He hung up.

He spoke so quickly that I didn't even have a chance to reply. I was trying to write the details down on the back of a flyer for pest control services, but I couldn't find a pen that worked and had to resort to memorising the address. It was already a quarter to two. If I wanted

14

to know what this was about, I'd better get a move on. The place wasn't far. I said a quick goodbye to Don Lalo and by three minutes to two I was already parking on the pavement of Avenida de la Américas. I located the gate under a long, tiled roof, flanked on either side by two modern buildings.

I rang the doorbell. A hook-nosed man stuck his head out of a little window and asked me what I wanted. He closed the window and let me into a shady, stone-floored entryway. The man, who had his thumb pressed over the end of a spurting hosepipe, indicated that I should head on in. The entryway was like a blind tunnel, with no windows or doors. The roof sloped ever higher and the air was damp and cool. In the distance, bathed in the midday sunlight, was a garden of papyrus plants and climbers. The ground gave way to a pond full of orange fish that you had to cross via a little path of mossy stepping-stones.

'Señor Horacio? Hello?' I called as I reached the other side of the garden, and found myself at the entrance to a dark hallway. My throat was dry with nerves. I went in. Through the smell of moths and age, I inhaled shellac, oil, beeswax.

My eyesight still hadn't adjusted to the darkness, so I could barely make out the shapes rising up on either side as I walked along. Piles of objects enveloped in cloth or bubble wrap. At the end of the hallway, a green lamp-shade drew a circle of light around a desk.

'Excuse me, I'm looking for Horacio Romero?' I moved closer. The man was on the telephone and when he saw me he signalled that I should take a seat opposite him and wait. He was both refined and abrupt. I heard him address someone in the same direct, brusque tone he'd used with me a few minutes ago: such-and-such is urgent, 'figure out a way to sort it out with customs, it doesn't matter how much it costs, those goods must come in immediately', and the like. It made me uneasy, all that impetuous urgency.

As I waited, my eyes grew used to the dark and I began to make out, with growing astonishment, the kind of goods the place was filled with: porcelain from who-knows-what dynasty, whole altarpieces extracted from some colonial church, polychrome Guatemalan carvings decorated with gold-leaf estofado. There were elephant tusks still smeared with mud and the dried flesh they'd been yanked from; slices of rare hardwoods two or three metres in length; books, piles and piles of old books; pieces of pre-Hispanic clay and limestone; gold-encrusted angels the size of men, carved from ebony; hawksbill turtle shells; wardrobes, tombs, folding screens with Indian marquetry, filigree and inlaid marble. A compact bundle tied up with twine didn't look like much at first, but eventually convinced me that all that excess – impossible to take in – was real: they were wild animal hides. A two-metre-high block of hides that had once roamed the jungle, the savannah, the desert, were now piled up like pigs' heads in a slaughterhouse. The value of the objects was incalculable. How do you put a price on time and memory? I imagined for a second that the objects were murmuring in the gloom and felt as if a prickly hand had grazed the nape of my neck.

I took refuge again in the island of light surrounding the desk. Horacio hung up the phone and stood briefly to greet me.

'You're the painter, right? I'm so glad you came, you don't know how pleased I am to meet you. It's hard to find good copyists these days.'

I also stood and took his hand, white and very soft, like a girl's. We sat down again.

'I need you to forge a painting for me.'

He came right out with it, brazen-faced. An alarm bell went off at once in my mind and I felt apprehensive. I didn't want to seem discourteous, though, so I kept listening.

'There's good money in it. If it turns out well I'll pay you handsomely. The problem is, it's a sixteenth-century panel. It's hard to persuade someone to take it on. It's too big.'

'A sixteenth-century panel? Who by?' I asked, with growing intrigue.

'It's a family relic. The museum value doesn't interest me much, but as far as I know it's attributed to Mabuse. Have you ever worked on a piece that old?'

I shook my head slightly, perplexed. 'And the copy... the forgery... what do you need it for?'

'To pass for the original, of course.' He smiled cynically.

'Sure, but who for?'

'For the heirs.'

I exhaled hard, like I was in the middle of a tough game of chess, and scratched my head. 'Ah, well, that complicates things. I'm sorry, I don't think I can help, Horacio.'

'What, you don't think a Mabuse panel can be forged?'

'No, I mean, it's not that I can't do it. It's just I don't like getting involved in that kind of thing, and from what you've said, well, it's complicated.' I leaned back in my chair and watched the fury flash across his face, like a Chinese dragon. 'Look, the truth is, a long time ago I got mixed up in something really bad, and after that I promised myself I'd never do forgeries again. To be honest, I don't even do copies these days. I'm working on my own paintings.'

His face softened. He propped his elbows on the desk and said, as if cajoling me, 'Of course, I hear you. I hear

17

what you're saying. In fact, that's why I went looking for you. I heard what happened with that politician. Respect, eh? Not everyone can make it all the way to a Sotheby's auction.'

'So you know what I'm referring to.'

'Of course. As Picasso used to say, true geniuses don't copy, they steal.'

'Right, the only problem is they lock you up afterwards.'

'Alright, alright, OK. With talent like yours, it must be hard not to be tempted by forgeries. Not many people can prove they're working at the level of the old masters…'

However manipulative Horacio's praise, I couldn't help feeling pleased. His words were drops of rain on dry earth, after all those arid months when everything had seemed to turn against me. I was grateful for his deference, though I didn't know if it was a good thing that my history had prompted him to seek me out. In any case, I declined his offer. I gave him a phone number for Felipe, a friend I'd worked with in Mendoza's studio. He was sure to accept. I got up to leave and held my hand out to him again.

'Think about it,' he insisted. 'I'd feel much better if you were the one to take this on. But either way, you'll have to show me your work. I don't usually buy directly for myself, but I could put you in touch with a couple of clients.'

I thanked him again and headed for the exit, where the sunlight had formed a shimmering triangle of floating dust particles. It had been two years since the incident Horacio had mentioned. In Mendoza's studio, we used to do restorations and back-up copies for museums run by the local council. It was common knowledge that Mendoza pulled tricks to rub shoulders with politicians and charm whoever was in charge of choosing the winning bids. But on that occasion it went too far. A government minister had asked him to forge a painting by Villalpando so he could take the original home. Felipe and I, the teacher's favourites, would be tasked both with making the replica and with swapping the pieces when it was done.

Mendoza invited us out for a drink, just us two: 'I know I can trust you boys.' He bought a couple of rounds and explained to us what the deal was. We nodded gravely, our faces appropriately solemn, taking our commitment to the boss to heart. It wouldn't be our first forgery, though we'd never had to deal with an outright theft. Mendoza knew how to spin it to make us feel important. He said things like, 'If this comes off well, we could partner up later on and make a lot more money,' or 'I trust you guys, I know I can count on your absolute discretion, even with the others in the studio.' Then when Felipe got up to go to the bathroom, he took the opportunity to tell me how much he was going to pay me and that, since he trusted me most of all, I would be in charge of the paperwork. We were there a long time, working out the details of the job. As maintenance workers, we'd have permission to come and go from the museum. Then Mendoza got up from the table saying he had to get home early, paid the bill and left the tab open: 'You guys celebrate for me, have whatever you like – you're single after all, make the most of it. Once you've got the old ball and chain, you're done for.'

Once we were a fair few drinks down, I mentioned I could use the money to finally pay off my truck. Felipe went pale and very serious, staring into his glass. He was my friend and knew exactly how much I still owed for it. Mendoza had offered him less than half the amount. Instead of falling out over it, we set to wondering how much Mendoza would be earning at our expense.

That was when it occurred to us to play the game in reverse. We'd do the forgery and go through with the whole farce of switching the paintings, but we'd deliver the fake one to the senator instead of the original. We knew the kinds of details we had to look out for so that even Mendoza wouldn't be able to tell the difference in the end. That night we left the cantina with our arms round each other's shoulders, swearing eternal friendship and believing ourselves the avengers of colonial art.

We carried out the whole plan, delivering the fake painting to the senator, even going so far as to install it in his home ourselves. Mendoza must have seen it hanging in the man's house at some politicos' dinner without realising it was the fake. The original, meanwhile, was still in its place in the museum.

Months later Felipe and I were arrested and made to confess that we'd forged the painting. The minister in question had been stupid enough to think he could auction off a piece by Cristóbal de Villalpando just like that. The valuers at Sotheby's figured out it was a fake and there was a huge scandal; since I'd signed the papers, I was the scapegoat. Mendoza paid my bail in exchange for my silence and for agreeing to keep myself at arm's length. I never heard from Felipe again.

I'd done my best to forget the whole story, but now that Horacio brought it up, all the details came back. I had to admit that the incident had done quite a number on me, and since then I'd struggled to regain my footing. I wasn't cut out for that kind of job any more. I needed to scrounge up whatever work I could and forget about painting once and for all. I wasn't prepared to go through something like that again.

In the street, the two o'clock sun hit me full in the face. I blinked a couple of times before realising the pavement was empty. My pickup had disappeared. My guts twisted as I saw, at the traffic light on the other side of the avenue, a tow-truck hauling it away. I tried running to catch up and beg the driver not to take it. I was prepared to hang off the moving vehicle, to stop it by any means necessary, then get down on my knees and plead for mercy: 'It's all I've got, please don't take it, I'll give you anything you want, I'll do anything as long as you don't take it'. Or at least allow me to unload Señora Chang's triptych so I'd have some way of paying the fine. But the traffic light went green before I could get to the corner and cross. In any case, I wouldn't have had anything to offer the driver, not even the paltriest bribe. I flapped my arms in despair, helplessly watching my sole possession disappear into the distance, and then stood there, feeling myself roasting in the sun, not knowing what to do. In the end I turned on my heel and headed back, defeated, to the big wooden gate. I rang a number of times and waited under the glare for what felt like an eternity before they opened up.

'You left me wondering. Could I see the painting?' I asked, back in front of Horacio's desk, trying desperately to conceal the anxiety that my face must have been showing. 'It's not every day you find someone in Mexico with a sixteenth-century panel, and I – '

'But of course, of course you must see it!' he exclaimed with the hint of a malicious smile.

'Just a look, that's all. I can't promise anything.'

'In truth, I'd appreciate your opinion,' he said, this time seriously. 'I have to admit I'm a total ignoramus when it comes to conservation and I want your advice.' He looked at his watch and got up from the chair. 'Are you hungry? My restaurant is just round the corner. It's one of the best in the city. Come, you're going to love the boeuf bourguignon.'

I'd never eaten in such a fancy place. I felt flattered by the invitation, but ashamed of the half-dirty work clothes

I was wearing. The maître d' greeted us and led us to what must have been Horacio's regular table. Both the maître d' and our waiter were careful not to frown over my appearance; doubtless they were wondering what the hell the owner of the restaurant was doing with a nobody like me.

Horacio ordered a series of dishes with strange French names, without even glancing at the menu.

'Put everything in the middle, and bring me a mineral water as well as my Cosmo, before you do anything else.'

'What can I offer you to drink, sir?' the waiter asked me, staring at his notepad.

'Which beers do you have?'

'Dark or light?'

'I'd like an Estrellita please.' I felt more and more humiliated and ridiculous. Instead of ordering wine, or tequila, or even a dark beer, I'd chosen the most ordinary thing possible for fear of straying from protocol. Not that Horacio seemed to care. I could see him more clearly now – his mannered, elegant body language, gelled hair, white gabardine trousers and moccasins.

'So tell me, I want to know everything about your career,' he said to me. 'Where were you born? Because you're not from Guadalajara, are you?'

I started telling him, in fits and starts, that I was born in Quiroga, Michoacán; that I was from a family of artisans; and that when I was very little a friend of my father's, who was a restorer working for the Viceregal Museum, had taken me under his wing.

'Mario!' Horacio called the waiter. 'Bring this gentleman a tequila from my cellar. And another Cosmo for me.'

After drinks, the platters of food appeared and I let myself soak up the succulent smells of olive oil, meat, basil and onion. The waiter served small portions onto our plates and we began to eat. It was the most delicious thing I'd ever had. The taste of those herbs, that butter, the soft meat melting on the palate.

'Now don't tell me you studied Visual Arts here,' Horacio said. 'I spotted your technique a mile off, and it's obvious you learned it abroad.'

'Actually, I get that mainly from my teacher. He did copies too, for museums and collectors. He was very sought-after. Perhaps you know him – Lorenzo Cruz.'

'Lorenzo… Lorenzo Cruz. No, never heard of him.'

'When he died, the National Institute of Anthropology and History put people from the department of conservation in charge of the museum, and so I came to Guadalajara.'

'Ah, their restorers are a total disaster. So that was when you began to study. Did you go to Florence, Milan?'

'Uh… yeah, a couple of months,' I lied. 'But to be honest I felt I was wasting my time with all that theory stuff. I mean, I know it's really important, but I already knew a fair bit from experience, and I needed work.'

'Tell me one thing, José.' He took a sip of his drink and leant closer to me, as if to tell me a secret. 'Do you know how to make a person blush?'

I felt myself suddenly start to sweat. I didn't know if it was an innuendo, a joke, or if he was actually referring to something I hadn't heard of. Horacio realised my discomfort.

'The *verdaccio* technique, man!' he said, laughing hard. 'Do you know how to paint rosy cheeks with *verdaccio crescendo* and *citronello grissini azurissimo*?'

'Ah, yes, of course,' I replied, overwhelmed. 'I watched Lorenzo use that technique several times, I know the process, though it's been a long time since I applied it.'

'Don't worry, there's barely a copyist left these days who uses it. It's enough that you know it. Only a good *verdaccio* will put the blush in *La Morisca*'s cheeks.'

23

I realised Horacio was taking for granted that I was going to accept the job. I wasn't sure whether or not I felt relieved, although to be honest I didn't have much of a choice. It would all come down to negotiating an advance.

'An excellent copyist is due to come here soon, the best of the best,' he said suddenly. 'He studied with the masters in Florence, a real genius. Even as a child he was copying Leonardos and Almedinas so perfectly that they started to call him Il Miracolo Torino. You'd love to meet him, I'm sure. I hope you'll agree to copy my *Morisca*. It would be the easiest thing in the world for him to do, but he's too expensive… Yes, far too expensive. Anyway, if we don't reach an agreement, I'll get in touch with your friend… What did you say he was called?'

'Felipe,' I said very quietly. My stomach had given another turn. I didn't know how much of what he said about the other painter was true, or whether Horacio had just said it to provoke me. What was certain was that if I lost this chance I'd literally be out on the streets.

The waiter returned for the empty plates and asked if we'd like coffee. I didn't usually drink coffee at that time of day, but all the tequila was starting to take its toll, including the warm Paloma I'd had in Don Lalo's shop. I ordered a strong americano, and Horacio an espresso and an apple tart with vanilla ice cream for us to share.

'So…? What happened exactly?'

'Hmm? What do you mean?'

'With the Villalpando. I want you to tell me everything, every detail.'

A clock rang out on the wall, alerting me to the time. It was half past three. If I wanted to try and get the rent money together, I needed to get out of there right now and come up with a plan. Or I could risk it with Horacio's forgery, assuming he decided to hire me and not the Miracolo Torino.

'What is it, man? Did I say the wrong thing?'

'No, no, sorry. I just remembered I have to deal with something.'

'But we're having such a good chat – I'm sure it can wait.'

'I forgot I need to go to the bank. I need to move some money so I can make a payment'. *The only way I could move anything in a bank right now would be if I robbed it at gunpoint*, I thought.

'You're really going to get up in the middle of our meal for a little thing like that? Come now, don't be rude. Don't you want to see the painting? Here… Mario! Bring me a notebook and a pen. I hope it isn't a fortune you owe, because if it is, you'll be my slave for life. Here…' He handed me the pen and paper. 'Write down who it is you need to pay, their account number or address or whatever, the exact amount and we'll send it to my secretary right away. You and I can settle up later.'

'No, Horacio, for goodness' sake! I can't let you – '

'Consider it a favour between friends.'

'But we barely know each other, Horacio, really, I can't go imposing like that.'

'Write! Now! You're starting to annoy me. And you don't know what I'm capable of, I won't put up with this kind of nonsense.'

He said this with such authority, and such menace, that I had no choice but to write down Doña Gertrudis's details and the number of months' rent I owed her on the notepad, plus a little more, to compensate for the delay.

'We'll sort it out later, don't you worry.' Horacio took the piece of paper, gave it a quick glance and handed it to the waiter. 'You'll pay me when you've had time to go to the bank, or in kind, I don't care. If you decide to paint the copy of *La Morisca*, I'll take it out of your advance.'

I smiled and thanked him, trying not to grovel.

'So, back to it then, tell me what happened with that Villalpando.' And I launched into the story in great detail.

We finished the coffee and the tart. The waiter brought over little glasses of orange liqueur which we knocked back in one go. Horacio excused himself to go to the counter and receive a call that seemed important. I was left alone at the table while Mario cleared away the last vestiges of our banquet. I imagined Doña Gertrudis receiving everything I owed her, probably in the form of a cheque, in a messenger's hands. The look on her face, and what she'd tell her nephew Panchito.

I got up to go to the bathroom, where I washed my face to try and liven myself up. I was starting to feel drunk. I looked at myself in the mirror: my hair and the neck of my shirt were damp, my eyes swollen. I realised I was letting the situation sweep me away like a dry leaf.

Horacio was waiting for me in the doorway. We headed to his car, a light blue Alfa Romeo parked outside the restaurant. It was boiling hot inside.

'You could bake a loaf of bread in here,' Horacio said as he moved the controls on the panel, and I imagined the dough swelling in the cup holder. The temperature gradually dropped as we sped away. I was very tired and kept nodding off, despite Horacio driving too fast, braking suddenly, pulling out quickly, running every traffic light he could, and overtaking where he shouldn't, including two or three police cars that didn't even seem to notice us. I'd later see that he had diplomatic number plates.

When we got to Avenida Acueducto, Horacio slammed his foot down. My stomach threatened to leap out of my throat with every dip in the road; this was what finally woke me. We slowed down as we moved along the shady, narrow streets of hilly San Javier. The houses were enormous. Each block had at most two or three properties. Everywhere there were trees and greenery;

high, very long walls, whitewashed or covered in neatly trimmed climbers; mossy pavements strewn with jacaranda, flame tree or bougainvillea petals.

Horacio slowed in front of one of these walls and turned up a ramp towards a garage door. To the side was a pedestrian entrance, guarded by two snub-nosed lions made of dark stone. The tiled eaves overhead suggested a colonial-style hacienda. Horacio clicked open the electric gate without getting out of the car. The tyres crunched on the pumice stone and then I was half-dazzled by the sun bouncing off a bare patch of ground. There was nothing there. It was just an empty lot, swarming with flies. I felt a little afraid. Horacio explained that the house was on the other side, so we left the car parked beside an old truck abandoned near a mound of sand, and crossed the empty lot, through thistles and spiny cardoons with pale yellow flowers.

On the far side of this parched wasteland, set into a perimeter wall, there was an unremarkable blue door. The pane of glass next to the lock was broken. Horacio stuck his hand through the hole and opened it, as though we were going to rob the place. He stepped aside to let me pass and I was swallowed up by a vegetal coolness that smelled like earth. My eyes took in the garden stretched out below. The different levels of the house stood out, pure white, among the jumbled green, cut out like a sign against the afternoon sky.

'What a beautiful house,' I exclaimed, astonished. 'And the garden... all this vegetation, it's like having your own jungle.'

'I'm glad you like it. The architect Luis Barragán designed it for my father. It's a kind of fortress made to guard his heirlooms. Mainly *her.*'

I noticed the high walls surrounding the house, only just hidden by the dense foliage.

'This here is the vault,' Horacio was saying, leaning against a wall that got higher as we descended some steps into the sloping garden. 'It'll blow your mind when you see all the treasures tucked away in here. Some of them are even older than *La Morisca*.'

To the right, a well-tended lawn followed the slope of the mountain. Further back, behind the silhouette of the house, the outskirts of the city could just be made out where they dissolved into sparsely populated plains, farmland and hazy hills growing yellow in the afternoon light. We'd reached the bottom of the steps.

'So your father is also an antiques collector,' I said, just to keep the conversation going.

'Oh, much more than that. Real collectors are so passionate they want to live the life of the objects in their possession.'

'How did you come to own *La Morisca*? It must have cost a fortune.'

Horacio was quiet as he deactivated the vault's security system. He opened the glass door and waved me in. It had a high ceiling formed of great oak beams, with a mezzanine advancing from the rear, leaving a full-height space by the entrance. The vault was illuminated by a tall window that formed an L-shape with the glass door. It felt like being inside a ship.

'It wasn't a matter of money, José. Perhaps you don't understand. Money debases art. None of what you'll find here was just bought in some antique market. And not a single piece in this collection could be put up for sale.'

I looked up. Both the mezzanine and the space below were piled high with pieces that should be in a museum, not jumbled there on top of each other.

'Of course, I understand,' I defended myself. 'I just meant it's unusual, even for a collector, to have such valuable objects here, so far from their places of origin, on another continent entirely, in a city like this where nobody would expect to find them.'

It was hard to pay attention to any particular object among that clutter of old wood and gold, like trying to find someone in a crowd. I could make out a samurai sword, a sextant, a sculpture of Krishna covered in ivory, three cat mummies, a glass case full of compasses, hourglasses, and incredibly old astronomical instruments... I felt dizzy.

There were two armchairs by the big window. I went to sit down while Horacio filled two glasses with a dark liquor he'd taken from a writing desk that had been repurposed as a bar.

'My father wasn't just a collector,' Horacio said, handing me one of the glasses. 'I mean, he wasn't just a brilliant art dealer, he also cared about the meaning of each heirloom. He went looking for its story, the meaning behind its value. And to that you had to add the long journey travelled by every object before it reached him, the circumstances of its acquisition. Or rather, the manner in which the object decided to belong to him. *La Morisca*, for example. Have you heard of Baron Sebottendorf?'

I shook my head.

'He owned the painting. He was a famous occultist, a good friend of Madame Blavatsky. They were looking for something like the entrance to an underground world inhabited by an ancient civilisation that paved the way for our own. He created an esoteric society that Hitler later twisted in order to found the National Socialist German Workers' Party. My father met the baron when he came to Mexico as Honorary Consul of Turkey, at a Masonic meeting his grandfather took him to. He was only sixteen, but his thirst for knowledge caught the baron's attention and won him over. I understand they wrote each other letters. Ten years later, they met again in Istanbul. By that time my father had quite a lot of experience in antiques. They called him the Golden Sleuth. He helped the baron get hold of dozens of old manuscripts, scrolls, rare books. And the baron shared discoveries and knowledge with him and no one else, so Papa ended up becoming his best disciple. Towards the end of the war, the baron decided to take his own life. He'd been passing information to the British, deceiving the Germans, persecuted by the Reich and at some point got stuck in the middle. He knew his knowledge and belongings were at risk of falling into the wrong hands, so before he jumped into the Bosporus he made my father promise to guard his most precious possessions: *La Morisca*, and the manuscripts and notes he had collected over the course of his life. Papa, faithful to his promise, loaded the baron's possessions onto a cargo ship owned by Blohm and Voss that was headed for the Port of Veracruz, along with the goods that would cement his prestige as an antiquarian and which were to fill his pockets for decades. And then he gave it all up to become a dervish.'

He ground out these last words through his teeth, saying them more to himself than to me. He took a single sip of the drink in his glass and fell silent, gazing somewhere over my shoulder. 'Here, come! I'm going to show you something.'

He stood abruptly and went out into the garden. I followed him into the undergrowth. Beneath the steps, carved into the rock of the hillside, was a niche, a metre and a half high, whitewashed like those little shrines you see by the side of the road. It was full of votive candles, saints' cards and artificial flowers covered in dust. At first I thought it was a funeral urn, but no. It was the mouth of a cave.

'One day, my father got it into his head to go into that hole, and I never saw him again,' he said, retrieving a key from beneath a millstone.

'You mean, he's...?'

'Alive? Of course not, this was ages ago.'

He crouched down to open the gate. He picked up one of the candles that had gone out, fiddled with the wick and blew inside the glass holder to clear it of dead leaves. He lit it and put it back in its place. He opened and closed the gate very carefully, just far enough for his hand to fit through, as though there was a bird inside waiting for its moment to escape.

'You know what? I feel like an absinthe. Come!' said Horacio, jumping up to return to the vault. 'Whenever I remember Papa, I feel like drinking absinthe, he used to love it. He was a very sophisticated man. It was a joy to watch him prepare it. I was still a child and I would sit on one side of the table, dumbstruck, watching the green fairy dance in the glass. And that smell! So delicious.'

I sat down again in the same armchair and watched him take various instruments out of the writing desk and place them on the coffee table: a glass bottle with a little bronze pourer, two glasses half full of a heavy liqueur the colour of dry leaves, a spoon with holes in it placed on top of each glass, and three lumps of sugar on the spoon. I couldn't imagine what all this paraphernalia was for. Each thing Horacio did or said seemed to be more extravagant than the last, and I was starting to get used to it. He opened the tap so the water dripped onto the lumps of sugar and dissolved into the drink.

'Watch,' he said, entranced. 'The green fairy... a woman with wings and long hair, who dances like those little ballerinas on music boxes, see?'

'Ah... yes, I think so.' In reality all I saw were the threads of alcohol forming whitish spirals as they mixed with the water. He took a long, silent drink. I saw him twist his mouth a little and I guessed the spirit was bitter.

'I have to confess I'm quite different to Papa,' he said then. 'He was wise, willing to sacrifice everything for knowledge. I'm just a simple merchant, a dealer, unscrupulous when it comes to putting prices on things. This you see here' – he indicated the stacks of accumulated objects – 'is something I'll never fully understand, I couldn't. I don't have the wherewithal to search so deeply. No, I want something much simpler.'

I didn't know what to say. He had a frank manner, like he was sharing truly personal things with me, and I had no way to reciprocate; my life didn't involve that kind of conflict. I set about finishing off my drink, so I could at least accompany him in that. The bitterness of the first sips made my throat tighten like a sharp wire pulled around my neck, which slowly began to ease until a soft, fragrant weight expanded over my chest.

I suddenly remembered something I hadn't thought of in a very long time: I was four or five years old, my brother and I were playing at my mother's dressing table in her bedroom, and we decided to prepare a concoction by mixing together her perfume with talcum powder and creams. We poured the concoction into a glass Manuel had stolen from the cabinet. The drink I had in my hand – it reminded me of the smell. We were arguing, my brother and I, about who would dare take the first sip, when we heard my mum coming and ran for cover. The house next door was abandoned, so I jumped over the fence to hide in there. My brother only managed to get as far as the wardrobe. I heard my mum telling him off from afar, and Manuel crying as she hit him. I was very scared. I went into the furthest room of the abandoned house. Inside a wardrobe was an empty trunk. Nobody would find me in there. I got into the trunk and as I pulled the lid closed the lock clicked shut. I tried to open it. I pushed with my back as hard as I could, but it was hopeless, it would only open a crack, which at least allowed me to breathe while I was inside. I screamed, but my own voice bounced off the walls and left me reeling. I waited hour after hour, sleeping in snatches, restless in my desperation, hungry, my muscles cramping. I thought I'd never be found, that I was doomed to remain there forever, dead, reduced to bones...

'You see?' Horacio interrupted my thoughts. 'Liquid magic. Give me your glass, I'll make you another.'

The first glass had been sickly sweet enough, and I was getting drunker. I sighed, gathering myself. I couldn't refuse.

'I'm really sorry about your father,' I told Horacio. 'It's clear you loved him very much. Losing him must have been tough.'

'Well, in fact, not at all. He tried to explain his reasons for becoming a dervish, why he needed to retreat from the world. He'd spend long periods of time inside the cave and I eventually got used to it. One day he simply never came out again. I was still very young at the time and didn't understand. I pictured his skeleton with a snake coming out of the eye socket. Sometimes I got it into my head that he was still alive. I'd have nightmares and wake up crying in the dark. I'd wonder if he was sitting stiffly in the lotus position or lying on the floor of the cave, shivering with cold, or scratching at the walls with his nails. The idea eventually faded as I grew up, until I forgot about it altogether. Then I travelled for many years and when I came back I barely thought about it at all. Like when there's a mouse in the house, and you know it's there, but you can't see it.'

I was still thinking about that trunk. A horrible shiver ran up my spine as I imagined myself in there, just as I'd ended up twenty-something years ago, scratching at the walls. I looked discreetly down at my nails. They'd been misshapen ever since.

'But cheer up, my man, I'll have none of that face. Shall we have some music?'

He opened a cabinet containing a rectangular gadget with blinking lights and a teetering stack of flat, transparent boxes. I'd never seen such a sophisticated device – I doubt they sell them in this country, it had to be from the US. Horacio placed three or four silvery disks into a tray that emerged from the machine. The soft thrum of a guitar immediately lightened the air and eased my nerves. The sky was cobalt blue. I concentrated on the music, on the house's peaceful atmosphere, and on the beautiful, smiling woman with translucent wings gazing up at me from the bottom of the glass.

2.

The next morning, I opened my eyes among cushions and silky sheets. I felt a warm weight by my feet. Lifting my head, I saw an enormous white bird, an albino peacock, which quickly rose, fanned out its entire tail and began to pick its way across my belly. Not yet strong enough to move, I lay there dumbfounded. The bird placed its feet on my chest. Its tail was a stunning white lace curtain in the morning light. It brought its beak to my face and cocked its head to fix me with a menacing yellow eye, ready to attack. I struggled desperately to get the thing off of me. I pressed my eyelids shut – and it was then I realised I was still asleep.

I woke again under the same grey silk sheets. Horacio's room was utterly silent. No one was there. I was naked except for my underwear – this detail being some cause for relief, considering I couldn't remember anything from the night before. I sat on the edge of the bed. The space was luxurious in a discreet, calculated way. *So this is what a rich antique dealer's bedroom is like,* I thought. Despite the quantity of absinthe I'd drunk, I didn't feel too awful. My clothes were scattered on the floor. I saw a slip of paper by my feet, folded in half: a cheque for a truly astronomical sum, written out to me.

The attempt to reconstruct the previous night caused me a sharp pain behind my left eye. I'd agreed to forge the painting and I hadn't even seen it yet. This cheque was just an advance. If the forgery passed for the original, Horacio would pay me double. Or at least that's what he'd said amid the drunken revelry. I had to see him right away. I tried to breathe through the throbbing in my head. I got dressed and stepped out into a corridor that fell away several stories to one side. The house was sunk in silence and I tried not to make any noise. I was barefoot, as I hadn't been able to find my shoes. The hallway led me toward the front of the house, with a view of the garden through an enormous picture window: the library, then the dining room, all decorated with exceptional care. Not a single false note. The style of the furniture, the bronze hues, the tribal pieces, the tapestries, the carpets.

I followed the distant hum of a radio: the recorded voice – 'At the third stroke, the time will be exactly…'– before the morning news. The hallway narrowed into a dark angle that reminded me of the stuccoed arcades at the pyramids.

I reached the kitchen. A woman wearing a traditional Zapotec dress from the Isthmus of Tehuantepec – a woven huipil blouse and a black velvet skirt, embroidered with yellow flowers, with a lace petticoat peeking out from below – was charring chillies on a griddle. Two grey plaits hung down her back, tied with yellow ribbons. On the other side of an L-shaped counter was a terrace teeming with lush vegetation. It was the same terrace I'd glimpsed yesterday evening through the window in the vault. I hoped to slip by unnoticed and avoid speaking with the cook, but the burn of the charred chillies made me sneeze.

36

'Jesus Christ!' the woman exclaimed in a surprisingly deep voice, whirling around in alarm. 'You nearly scared the wits out of me. And who might you be, young man?'

'I'm sorry, hello,' I said, cowed. 'I'm a painter. Horacio hired me to copy a painting.'

'I see… Have a seat, my boy. Coffee?"

'Thanks.'

'Yes thanks or no thanks?'

'Yes, yes, please.'

On closer look, I realised that the cook must be a muxe, that third gender from down in the Isthmus, who behave and dress like women. The terrace had a metal table and some chairs, all enamelled in bottle green. I was about to sit when I heard a splash coming from the garden. It was Horacio, swimming laps in the pool. I walked over to the edge. A fine layer of steam covered the water's surface and the tips of the hanging plants swayed with the ripples.

The cook placed a mug of coffee on the counter. I blew on it before taking a sip. I stood there for a few moments, watching Horacio's pale, athletic form against the navy-blue tiles. After a few more laps, he finally emerged from the water, pulled on a plush robe and made for the kitchen without so much as a glance in my direction.

'Tona, you can bring breakfast out now, and tell El Gordo to join us. Have you met José? He's going to be working here at the house, so I want you to treat him like one of the family, OK?'

'Of course. You know me, always giving the young master's guests the royal treatment.' The cook flashed me a malicious smile from the other side of the counter. I felt a strange sense of menace, as if she might attack me at any moment – but only behind the boss's back.

'Right. Come on,' Horacio said to me, 'let's go to the chapel so you can see the painting.'

I put down my coffee and followed him to the rear of the terrace. The masonry perimeter wall formed a right angle here with another, even higher one. So much humidity was trapped in this corner that tiny wild ferns sprouted from the cracks.

Horacio stopped at a narrow, heavy door. The wood was swollen and the hinges had buckled under the weight. He struggled with the lock and heaved his shoulder against the door until it swung open just enough for him to slip through. I followed him. It was dark inside. A deep, cavernous echo suggested that the space was nearly empty. I felt around for a light switch. The air smelled of tallow and salt. The cold of the ground seeped into my feet.

'I can't find the switch,' I told Horacio.

'There's no electricity in here. In a moment we'll have El Gordo open the shutters.'

His voice reached me from the farthest corner. I heard the rasp of a lighter. Horacio lit the wick of a candle as stout as a tree trunk, and the flame brought out the hazy outlines of the space: a long box, some twenty metres deep, six high and six wide. Set into the back wall was a relatively simple altarpiece with estofado detailing. Horacio lit two more candles. The flames illuminated the space enough for me to make out the marvel that stood before me: *La Morisca*.

The panel was set about one and a half metres off the ground. I drew closer, growing more and more astonished by the beauty of the composition, until my face was all but pressed to the surface. It was extraordinary. Two metres wide by three metres high. By candlelight, the colours gained a weight and a depth that made my chest tighten. I felt as if it were the first time I was looking at a real painting, as if I'd never seen anything so beautiful. So many years had passed since I'd worked with my teacher that I'd quite forgotten the feeling of standing face to face with an ancient piece, without museum lighting, without a line to keep me from getting too close and touching the craquelure, smelling the age of the materials, detecting the brushstrokes under the layers of glazing and the patina. It was like pushing past the imposture of sanctity and stepping into the painting itself, taking hold of it, of all the genius that lay behind the image and served like a precision mechanism: the gears of a clock that had been hidden for hundreds of years but never stopped ticking.

'*Young man, do not look too long at that painting, or you'll sink into despair*', said Horacio, breaking the spell.

'Huh?'

'That's what a Balzac character says to a young man as he stares at a work of art. By Mabuse, to be precise. The *Adam*. Do you know it?'

Confused, I shook my head. I wasn't sure if he was talking about a book or a painting or something else altogether.

'Of course, since you have to copy it, you'll have no choice but to sink into despair,' he said, and laughed. Horacio was perched on a rough-hewn wooden desk, much like the ones used by monks in the Middle Ages for copying manuscripts.

'Mabuse, as in Jan Gossaert, Mabuse? Didn't he paint a *Virgin with Child* holding an apple in his hand?'

'That's the one. You've seen it!'

'Yes, it's at the Prado,' I lied. I hadn't seen it, only a picture in a book, and I remembered that the caption had said it was on show there. It had clearly made quite an impression for me to still remember it after all that time.

'Dürer said Mabuse was nothing but an artisan with good intentions,' Horacio said, propping up his feet on the desk. 'The nerve. They never understood his real genius: producing the error, the incidental stain, far

39

more unsettling than the clumsy naturalism of Flemish painters or those little games of hidden symbols and all that nonsense Dürer himself was so taken with. But like I said, it's only an attribution. There's no signature or irrefutable proof that Mabuse is the painter, other than the nature of the brushstroke – which is unmistakable – and the fact that the timing makes sense, and the geographical references... The truth is, though, that it could be any other painter of that era.'

I stepped back a bit to take in the whole. Horacio stopped speaking and once again I was overcome with astonishment at the painting. In the foreground was the woman, dressed in a luxuriantly draped blue overgown; the cloth was flecked with stones sparkling like constellations, the skirt trimmed with gold filigree. Unlike most Renaissance paintings, La Morisca's features strayed from the European ideal: olive skin, heavy brows, large and slightly almond-shaped eyes, full lips, dark hair. Seated in three-quarter view, the woman stared straight at the spectator, holding a pearly, opaque, seemingly weightless sphere in a perfect demonstration of the golden ratio. Behind her stood the ruins of a classical structure, columns and capitals invaded by weeds. Beyond the ruins was the landscape, lit by sunlight filtering through the treetops. Suddenly I felt Horacio's breath at my neck, inhaling deeply, and I jumped away in surprise.

'So who was La Morisca?' I asked nervously.

'You mean the woman?' he said with the hint of a cynical smile. 'No one in particular, as far as I know. I expect she's the symbolic representation of a concept, like the sculpture of Justice. I mean, she isn't Justice or Liberty or anything like that, it's far more complicated. I never really understood what the whole business was about. Papa gave me some vague explanations, but I don't remember much. The name of the painting isn't on record, either. That's what Papa called her for as long as I can remember, but it's just our way of referring to her... Now, if you want to figure it out, all you'll have to do is study this lot' – he gestured to the towering bookcase at his back, piled with rolled up parchments and leather-bound tomes behind a locked metal grate – 'assuming you know Hungarian, Old German, Latin, Greek...'

I was growing more intrigued by the minute, though my mind swirled with questions. I sat on a long bench up against the wall, wondering what could be in all those old papers, what light they might shed on *La Morisca*. I looked at the painting again from that angle. It was going to be a colossal job. I'd never attempted anything like it before.

'Let's go, you'll have plenty of time to look at it. Here's the key. Always lock up on your way out. No one else can ever come in here, understood?'

Outside, on the terrace, the sun filtered through the bougainvillea and passionflower vines. I squinted, dazzled. We sat at the table and La Tona served us each a heaped plate of chilaquiles and shredded chicken. In the middle of the table she placed a basket of bread, the pot of coffee, and some exquisitely fragrant grilled sausages. Ravenous, I tried to eat with as much dignity as I could muster, making proper use of my cutlery, taking slow, small bites. I felt ridiculous, but Horacio seemed naturally graceful and I didn't want to come off poorly. My mind began to buzz with plans for the forgery.

'So, what do you think? Can you have it ready in three months?'

'What?' I blurted, horrified.

'Two and a half would be ideal, really. I can't risk something going wrong. I've already got everything arranged with customs, the heirs and the lawyers.'

'No, Horacio, it's not enough time. A job like this has to be approached so carefully. You have to mix the pigments, age all the layers of glazing, standardise the details…'

'But yesterday you said yourself that it wouldn't be a problem.'

I cursed inwardly. I'd got so drunk I didn't remember saying any of that.

'Copying the piece, sure,' I hedged. 'But it's not just about copying the piece. I have to forge the panel itself, create the effects of damp and termite damage where necessary, apply a chemical treatment to make the fibres look as corroded as they are in the original…'

'Forget about all that. We'll do it *à la Chaudron, mon chéri*.'

'À la what?'

'Like Chaudron, who forged the *Mona Lisa*. We'll use a panel from the same period. You have no idea how hard it was to find a poplar panel that big.'

'Oh, right,' I said with some relief, 'that will help. Mostly it'll save us time. But we still have to figure out what to do about the heirs. What kind of authentication will they be doing, do you know?'

'Don't worry. I was the one who suggested returning the painting in exchange for a small favour. They trust it's in good faith. As long as they recognise it by sight, we're fine. Unless it arouses suspicion, I'm sure they won't order lab tests or anything like that.'

'I don't know, Horacio. I think it's going to be really tough, even so.'

'So now you're telling me you're backing out?' His cutlery clattered onto the plate. 'I made a commitment and I need to honour it. Now you're going to say you don't feel up to the task or something equally stupid. I hope you understand that there's far too much at stake here, José.'

'That's exactly why I don't want to let you down. I'm

42

not saying it's impossible, just that it'll take a lot of work, and that means time.'

'Oh, please! That advance I paid you is enough to achieve the impossible. You'll find the time.'

I felt like my stomach was on fire. *It's not about money*, I wanted to snap back; *money debases art*, just as he'd said the day before. But I held my tongue. I had no choice. He'd got me out of a tight spot and I felt obligated to hold up my end of the bargain.

'Alright. Don't worry,' I told him solemnly. 'I'll figure out a way to get it done in three months. It'll happen, even if I have to work morning, noon and night.'

'That's what I like to hear! You'll have access to everything you need. Gordo!' He called to a man at the edge of the pool. He was down on all fours, scooping leaves out of the filter. He stood up and came over to the table. He was wearing khaki overalls – too tight around his middle, too short at the hem – and a pair of mud-stained industrial boots.

'The studio needs a good cleaning. José's going to be working there.' Horacio nodded in my direction. 'Help him with whatever he asks, please. And I need you to go upstairs and open the shutters in the chapel.'

El Gordo nodded, his eyes fixed on the ground. He turned and went back to collect the equipment he'd been using to clean the pool. Horacio pushed his plate to the centre of the table, took a pineapple empanada, broke it in half and took a bite from the middle before tossing it back into the basket.

'I have to go out and I'm already running late,' he said with his mouth full of pastry. 'I'm going to get changed. Take a look at the studio in the meantime. Tonight we'll discuss what's missing.'

He got to his feet and walked off. A gecko appeared on the table and began to pick at the crumbs.

The studio was located at the back of the property, separated from the house by a ten-metre expanse of lawn. It was a sort of cabin: facing the garden, the front façade was all glass, sheltered from the sun by a tiled overhang and the canopy of a pepper tree with a twisted trunk. I found my shoes by the door, my socks rolled up inside them.

The studio appeared to have been used as the junk room. It was crammed with boxes, obsolete appliances, old clothes. El Gordo was dusting off objects and piling them up in a corner, tossing the rubbish into a sack. In the centre of the room, leaning against the wall, was what must have been the panel for the forgery, covered with a blue plastic tarp. Beside it was a large table and several shelves bursting with paint cans, expired materials, stiff brushes, hessian and tools of every kind.

There was a door on the right side of the studio. I thought it must be a closet, but when I opened it, I discovered that it was actually a small bedroom. Though austere in comparison to the opulence and scale of the house, it had all the essentials: a nice bed, a bathroom with a tub, far more than the trappings of my own wretched flat. I was especially happy about the bathtub. It was white, with a bronze tap and feet. I'd always wanted one, always daydreamed about soaking in hot water for hours. A pleasant wood-framed window offered a view of the garden from the bath. I thought of asking Horacio to let me sleep here once in a while instead of coming and going from my flat, so I could finish the forgery on schedule. I was sure he wouldn't mind.

The space was perfect, although it screamed to be salvaged from grime and neglect. I started by clearing the table and shelves. I laid out the tools and various other bits and pieces that could still be useful. Next I filled two sacks with old papers, rags, beer bottles, tubes of dried paint and assorted junk, and as I did so I made a list of everything I'd need for the forgery.

Then I set out to clean the bedroom, asking El Gordo for a bucket, a scouring pad and some Pinol floor cleaner, but he didn't seem to understand what I was saying. He just stood there blankly, his pupils restless, eyes drifting to one side or trained on the floor. I figured he must have some kind of mental disorder. I tried to explain myself through gestures, but to no avail. I gave up. I'd speak to La Tona later. I kept inspecting the containers of solvents and old paint tubes, and just when I'd put the whole thing out of my mind, I discovered that El Gordo had brought in everything I'd asked for and was already cleaning the bathroom. He mopped the floor, changed the sheets, removed anything that was broken. He left the place as spotless and comfortable as a hotel room.

Around noon, Tona appeared with a tray of guacamole, cuts of beef, salsa, tortillas, and a pitcher of lemonade. She left it on the table I'd just cleaned: 'Here's a bite to eat. Enjoy,' she said, before disappearing again. Seeing them together made me realise how strong the resemblance was: their facial features, their build. I thought they might be twins: La Tona draped in traditional skirts and covered in makeup, El Gordo dressed like a prisoner, unable to make eye contact. Like two radically different versions of the same person.

I polished off a glass of lemonade in one go and poured myself another. My head swarmed with plans and ideas for everything I'd have to do to finish the copy before the deadline. Three months wasn't nearly enough, even when painting on an original panel. But without one, there was no way it could be done. I could have spent months ensuring the warping and the termite damage looked right. Creating the buckles and cracks almost always yielded unexpected results, and you'd have to start all over. I eyed the blue tarp warily as I ate. I'd been avoiding the issue this whole time, not wanting to see the painting I'd have to erase.

I tugged at the cloth and it fell to the ground. My blood ran cold. It wasn't a sixteenth-century panel, it was fifteenth-century. I was sure of it. Five hundred years ago, someone had depicted a human figure: David before becoming king. A shepherd with his staff, a sheep in tow, his saddlebag filled with stones to scare off the wolves trailing his flock. Someone had used colour and technique to depict the world as humans used to see it, without television, without abstractionism, without the Renaissance.

It wasn't just that I now grasped what it would mean to erase a painting of incalculable historical value. Despite the white gaps of the craquelure and the heavy patina, I'd realised right away that I was looking at none other than *that* painting: the Berruguete that had been part of an exhibition at the Museo de Bellas Artes some twenty years prior. Don Lorenzo, my teacher, had taken the trouble to bring me to the capital city and give me a detailed lecture on Renaissance painting. He'd used this very panel as an example of the Flemish School's 'discovery' of volume.

Days later, back in Tepotzotlán, we heard that the painting had been stolen from the museum warehouse and its whereabouts were unknown. Don Lorenzo lamented the robbery for months and followed the news as if a close relative had been kidnapped. He'd cut out all the articles he could find about the theft and pin them up on a bulletin board with other important papers. The photo that the newspaper had released to announce the robbery, printed in black and white, looked far more like the actual painting than the ruined vestige I had in front of me today.

I covered the painting again, just as all that time ago I'd covered Don Lorenzo's marble-white face with a blanket when I found him face down in the studio. My eyes welled with tears. Erasing that painting would mean erasing a memory of him. Although, truth be told, time had done its work on both my memory and the painting itself. What remained was a wreckage.

I'd hung my keys on a nail by the panel. The keychain was a coiled-up metal snake that had belonged to Don Lorenzo. That snake was a kind of amulet for me, a silent sign of his presence.

Horacio returned around six o'clock with a bottle of champagne and two glasses.

'You've certainly done justice to the place,' he said, looking around. He took a seat.

I'd arranged a little sitting room by the picture window. I brought in a couple of Miguelito armchairs I'd found in a stack, pushing a squat table with wrought-iron legs into the centre. The space felt really homely. The freshly mopped clay-tiled floor gave off a cool and earthy air. Twilight fell. The only light I'd left on was an architect lamp I'd dug up from one of the boxes and clamped onto the edge of the work desk.

Horacio uncorked the champagne and poured.

'Welcome,' he said by way of a toast. He stood and began to inspect the newly organised shelves. 'As I'm sure you've deduced, my father used to paint here. Apparently he was quite good, though it was only ever a hobby for him. Who knows where his paintings ended up.'

'I would've liked to see his work,' I said, just to make small talk. I was exhausted.

'Did you fix up the bedroom, too?' he asked, peering through the open door.

'Yes, El Gordo cleaned in there as well.'

'Good. You can sleep here, if you like. Make yourself right at home, my friend. Whatever you need.'

He paused and looked me up and down. 'Come on, bring the bottle. We could both use a decent soak.'

We entered his bedroom through the garden. I followed him into a changing room, where he stripped down unhesitatingly. I stalled, averting my eyes, staring at the varnished wood shelves full of elegant clothing. He had over thirty pairs of shoes, all neatly arranged. Neckties in every colour.

'I'll wait for you to get changed. Here, you can wear these.'

I accepted the swimming trunks Horacio offered me as he took the champagne bottle from my hand. He walked through a door at the back of the changing room. Through the crack, I could see a dressing table covered in little perfume bottles. I placed my glass on a shelf to strip down, leaving my clothes strewn on the floor beside Horacio's. The trunks were a tight fit.

Inside, steam softened the atmosphere. It was a large, marble-panelled room with bronze and burnished wood trim. Horacio was testing the water and adding bath salts. I got a full-on view of him without his towel and lowered my eyes. I felt more like I was looking at a woman than at a sophisticated thirty-something man.

On a raised platform a few feet high were two tubs, one larger than the other. In the bigger one, a pair of lion masks spewed boiling water. The second, ringed by plants, was freezing and lined with river stones on the bottom. Between the two tubs was a marble divan. The stone emulated the softness of upholstery and folds of cloth.

Horacio rinsed himself off under a shower beside the platform. Once he was done, I did the same. I scrubbed off the sweat and grime with soap so I wouldn't soil the water in the tub. We eased our way in. The water was too hot, but I felt my muscles and nerves relaxing deliciously. We sat there in silence, submerged, motionless. I listened to the glassy echo of a drip every couple of seconds and gazed up, stunned, at the Mudéjar filigree dome, just like in the Alhambra. It felt like staring into an endless tunnel.

Horacio abruptly rose out of the pool and said it was time for the first switch. He sat on the divan and then lowered himself into the tub of cold water for a few moments. I didn't in the slightest feel like following him, but I supposed it had to be good for you, so I resolved to give it a try. Meanwhile, Horacio got down from the platform and disappeared before returning with a plate of dates, olives, cheese cubes and quince jelly.

I got into the tub of cold water and couldn't keep my face from twisting into a cowardly grimace.

Horacio was amused. 'Don't tell me you've never been in a hammam before.'

I shook my head, shivering, and immediately retreated to the hot water tub.

'Ah, you've no idea the wonders a change in temperature can reap. Here, look.' He splashed some hot water onto the marble divan. 'Lie down on your belly.'

I obeyed, arranging myself as comfortably as I could. Horacio rubbed an oily, intensely fragrant lotion into his palms and began to massage my back muscles with gestures as light and rhythmic as waves in a lagoon. I was nodding off when he gave me a couple of slaps on the flabby part around my middle.

'All right, my turn. Gently, eh. Don't go cracking any joints.'

I complied, massaging Horacio's fragile ribcage. I slipped my oily hands over his mottled skin, its freckles and red moles. I feared that even the slightest touch might hurt him. I tried to appear distant, impersonal. But I soon heard his breath growing heavier and I felt nervous. As if absentmindedly, he dropped a hand into the water and grazed my inner thigh. I leapt as if I'd seen a poisonous snake under the water and plunged backward; a wave rose up over the edge and the champagne bottle fell to the bottom of the tub. Horacio, entertained by his own joke, let out a riotous guffaw and rolled over, dropping into the cold water. He emerged looking thoroughly smug. I picked up the bottle, now filled with both water and champagne, and set it down on the edge. He poured two glasses of cognac and left one by my hand, but I didn't feel like drinking any more – my guard was up. He raised the champagne bottle as if to read the label and smiled.

'Sorry, it was an accident,' I said, rather grudgingly.

'Oh, don't you worry, that's what it's for.' He turned it upside down and poured the contents straight into the tub. He took a sip of cognac and stretched out calmly on the marble divan.

'I'm taking a trip. I'll be gone for a month or so, maybe two. There's no reason why I should tell you this, but I thought it might interest you. There's an antiques forger in Beijing who's offered me shares in his company if I help get his merchandise into Europe. If, after you've finished forging *La Morisca*, you want to try your luck on the other side of the world, I could put in a good word for you. I'm sure he'd hire you sight unseen for a sum you won't get here in a million years. Once we clear the way, business will skyrocket like you wouldn't believe.'

'You've sorted it out with customs already?' I asked, trying to hide my excitement at the thought of travelling to China.

'Yes, well, that's the other part where you'd come in. The thing is, the route is easier by sea, naturally. Across the Indian Ocean and then the Suez Canal to dock in Italy. As you can imagine, customs are awfully strict there. They demand a ridiculous number of licenses, certificates...'

'Right...'

'I spent a long time trying to figure out how to get in. I got in touch with all sorts of port directors until I learned, entirely by chance, making small talk at some soirée, that the wife of the *ministero degli affari esteri* was none other than... guess who?'

'No idea.'

'The granddaughter of the Baron! Rudolf von Sebbotendorf himself! Can you believe it? As if orchestrated by fate. The woman is obsessed with recovering her grandfather's assets, so I quickly figured out a way to cross paths. I found her at the Semenzato auction, where I bid a couple of times to catch her attention and then let her win. I approached her afterwards to offer my congratulations and make a toast. It wasn't hard to find a way of bringing up the paintings that went missing after the war. She told me about her grandfather's collection. I feigned surprise and said I knew "someone" who had a rare sixteenth-century panel with such-and-such characteristics. I said I'd heard it came from Istanbul and had belonged to the adopted son of a nobleman. She immediately knew it was *La Morisca*. Since "ethics" prevented me from revealing the name of the alleged owner, I stressed my willingness to mediate in the negotiations and delivery of the piece. We became great friends. I told her about my situation and what I needed for the business I was about to start with my Chinese partner, and so she had no choice but to offer me her husband's help in return. He and I now have an excellent relationship, by the way. One can't help but fall in love with such pleasant, courteous people. They're absolutely top-tier.'

Listening to Horacio, I watched him refill his glass again and again, while I merely wet the tip of my tongue with the liquor. He got as drunk as the night before, or worse. He started blathering on about how he didn't want to be just some rich daddy's boy. Ranting now, he insisted that he wanted to make something of himself, that he'd rather give it all up than fall back on his father's prestige. Stuff like that.

The water had cooled and I started to feel chilly. I got out of the tub and slipped into a bathrobe I found among the clean towels piled up on a shelf. I also brought Horacio a silk robe from its hook on the back of the door and helped him put it on. By this point he could barely stand and was babbling absolute nonsense. I dragged him toward the couch in his bedroom, where he curled up and fell asleep.

By contrast, I felt more energetic than ever; the bath had perked me up and made me hungry. I wolfed down the entire tray of cheese and dates. I also found a tin of pâté in the minibar, which I ate on Ritz crackers as I poked around Horacio's room. I sniffed the little bottles of perfume, pulled his silver brush through my hair, studied the labels on imported products and tried to decipher the Russian, German and Japanese. How could one man possibly need so many cosmetics and creams, I wondered.

I thought I should probably make my way back to the studio bedroom. I saw that Horacio was shivering under his blanket. I didn't want to rouse him and put him to bed, so I pulled the quilt off the mattress and arranged it over his sleeping body. I cast around for something to read until I felt tired enough to sleep, and that was when I recognised the leather-bound folder Horacio had been carrying around that afternoon. He'd set it on top of some shelved books. Without giving it much thought,

I opened it. Maybe I wanted to make sure that Horacio was who he said he was, that some of the wild tales he'd told me were true.

There was the plane ticket from Guadalajara to Los Angeles and from Los Angeles to Beijing, along with an informational pamphlet on luxury holiday options in Thailand, annotated in blue pen. The passport, slipped into the pocket on the other side of the folder, said his full name was Raúl Horacio Romero Lomelí, and that he was thirty-eight years old. The little green passport was worn with use and full of stamps from different countries. There was also a folded manila envelope full of money, accompanied by a handwritten note. Among the incomprehensible scribbles was my name.

3.

I stayed up very late, leafing through a book of Mudéjar architecture, my body still imbued with a pleasurable sensation from the bath. The sun was already high in the sky when I woke. I remembered Horacio was going travelling and rushed out to see if I could catch him. I tied the belt of my bathrobe as I crossed the garden and then peered into his bedroom through the sliding glass door. Inside, it wasn't just untidy – it looked like the place had been ransacked. He seemed to have packed at the last minute, throwing whatever he could find into a suitcase before he left. There were drawers emptied out onto the floor, clothes flung all over the place. The leather folder was open, empty, on the desk.

I found one of my shoes under the bed and the other by the door of the wardrobe. I put them on then and there, without socks. My clothes were no longer where I'd left them. I felt a rush of dread and the blood drained from my face. *This cannot be happening*, I thought. I'd forgotten to take the cheque out of my shirt pocket. Alarmed, I went into the kitchen. Tona wasn't there. I heard a rhythmic, mechanical noise on the other side of the pantry and feared the worst. Hearing my footsteps,

Tona came down a narrow spiral staircase from the staff quarters and found me staring at the washing machine.

'Morning, lost something?'

'My shirt. A checked shirt I left in Horacio's room, have you seen it?'

'There are clean clothes in your room for you to use. You really think I'd let you go round day after day in those same old stinking rags?'

'It's… the cheque, my payment, it was in the pocket of my shirt – you must have seen it. Did you take it out?'

'Cheque? I didn't see any cheque.' She came over and shouldered me aside, but before she could stop me I pulled open the lid and the cycle came to a stop. I cast around in the water for my shirt, then pulled it out, dripping, and extracted a lump of wet paper from the pocket.

'Here it is, see? This was my cheque!' I said, trying to contain my anger. I threw the pulpy clod to the floor.

'Ah, well, I never saw it. I suppose you expect me to go feeling around in strangers' underwear, do you?'

'But I never asked you to wash my clothes, you took them without permission. This was my payment for the work I'm doing for Señor Horacio. How am I supposed to get anything done now…?'

'Well, what do you expect me to do about it? It's not my fault you people leave your dirty things lying around because you're always in a rush.'

I tossed the shirt back into the water, slammed the lid shut and left, raging. I went to the studio and tried to calm myself down, but all I wanted was to get the hell out of there. My stomach was smouldering. I needed to get dressed and take off. I found a pile of clean clothes on a chair in the bedroom and pulled on a pair of stiff trousers and a cotton shirt. I strode right across the garden and the empty lot without a backward glance.

Once I was in the street, I had the feeling I'd forgotten something, and patted my pockets. But what could I possibly have forgotten, if I didn't even own anything? All I had were my keys, which I'd reflexively grabbed before leaving.

Seeing as I didn't have a single coin on me, I had to walk the long route home from Colinas de San Javier. The sun seared my skin and the soles of my shoes were melting. Damn you, Tona. I could be at the bank by now, enjoying the air conditioning and receiving preferential treatment from an executive in a suit and tie. I would have left with a wad of bills tucked into my waistband and taken a taxi to pick up my truck from the pound. Instead, I was trudging uphill along the entire length of Avenida Revolución, and on an empty stomach, too.

That said, the walk did help me collect myself. I'd get home, tell Doña Gertrudis I'd be out of town for a few days, pick up some materials and head back to Horacio's house. I was going to have to ask her to lend me a few pesos for the bus back, which was embarrassing, but she could hardly refuse me so little after I'd paid back everything I owed – on time, no less, plus a bit extra to compensate.

On further consideration, I realised it had been pretty immature of me to get so wound up about the cheque. Not that it mattered what Tona thought of me. She was only doing her job. I'd talk to Horacio and ask him to write me another cheque or pay my advance by some other means. My truck would have to wait.

I knew something was wrong before I even reached home. I could see flowered curtains through the windows. I'd never put curtains up. There was a sign on the glass panel of the door – THIS IS A CATHOLIC HOME – and the key wouldn't turn in the lock. I went to the rear of the building, ran up the mildewy stairs and knocked on Doña Gertrudis's door. A young girl opened, dressed in her school uniform, and I asked for her grandmother. The stink of damp and garlic turned my stomach. The girl glanced back inside the apartment and answered robotically that she wasn't home. I asked when she was expected to return, and she looked round again; she didn't know, she said. I was about to blast a stream of expletives at the poor girl for being a scheming little liar, but I contained myself. I realised I was about to vomit. I barely made it down the stairs before I had to crouch down and let out a stream of bitter saliva into the potted mallows.

When I stood up, who should I see but Panchito, leaning in a dark doorway behind me with his arms crossed, smiling.

'What are you doing here, dickhead?' he asked, the smile still fixed on his face.

'That's my sofa!' I pointed behind him.

'Which sofa? There's nothing of yours here.'

Then the great hulking figure grabbed me by the back of the neck and yanked me violently, easily, towards the exit, like a scrawny cat. I flew through the air, then felt every bone of my back slam onto the ground.

'You show up here again and I'll break your fucking neck. You hear me?' He rounded things off with a kick to the gut that knocked me further away from the gate. I writhed, winded, on the pavement.

A fat woman emerged from what had once been my apartment.

'What's going on, Pancho?'

'You stay out of this! Close that door!' he shouted, as though about to hit her too.

I groped around on the ground to heave myself up.

'I don't want you within thirty metres of this place, you hear me?'

I nodded. He turned on his heel and I watched him go up to his aunt's flat. I took a couple of lurching steps away, holding onto the wall. One of my stretcher frames was leaning at the base of a tree, and further along I found a box of my clothes, drenched, sitting in a puddle. I tipped it over with my toe. On the corner, a couple of kids were playing with my box of paints. I gave one of them a smack before snatching it off him, and he fled into his house in tears. I ran off as quickly as I could, hugging the box to my chest.

I stopped to catch my breath at Parque Morelos, exhausted. I drank from a pump and stretched out on a bench, hugging my paint box like I was floating out on open water and this was the last relic of my sudden shipwreck. The mahogany box was colour-stained, a bit battered from heavy use, but sturdy. It was mine, could only have been mine. Stupid brats, I should have hit them harder. By the time I was their age I was spending my afternoons cutting and sanding the wooden pieces of that box, following Don Lorenzo's instructions to slot each one into place.

I started to wonder what the hell could have happened. Perhaps Horacio's secretary had forgotten to pay or had somehow misplaced the piece of paper with the details I'd given her boss. Perhaps Doña Gertrudis hadn't wanted to take the cheque – or worse, the ungrateful thief had taken the cheque, kept the money and still chucked my things out into the street. Perhaps Horacio had lied to me.

I lay motionless for a long while, sprawled on the bench, trying to piece it all together, but I could do no more than speculate. In the end, I had no alternative but to retrace and wait for Horacio to return from his trip so we could settle up. I started making my way back in the hottest part of the afternoon, my insides still twisting.

When I finally reached the gate flanked by those two snub-nosed lions, I realised there was no way to get in. There was no doorbell or handle or anything like it. The pedestrian entrance was just a single metal sheet, completely smooth, as was the door to the garage, which was activated via remote control. I knocked as hard as I could, using my palm, my fist, my keys, but there was no way I'd be heard all the way across the empty lot and the garden. Desperate, I started kicking at the door, fuming with rage, when I heard a police car behind me. Two brief wails of a siren and the roar of a V8 engine.

The police van went up the ramp to the garage, cutting me off. Two officers got out and hemmed me in against the wall. One of them seemed more zealously authoritative and began to interrogate me.

'Come on then, you gonna tell us what the hell you're doing kicking in the door to this house?'

He was thin and stringy looking, but with the attitude of a burlier man. The other one, flabby and older and wearing a cowboy hat, stood a little way off.

'I work here, officer. I was knocking for them to let me in. You see, there's no doorbell, and the staff are really far away...'

'As if there's no doorbell. You hear that, pal?' the stringy one said to the older cop. 'You do know this is Colinas de San Javier, right? All the houses have doorbells here, and security systems. They even have cameras, did you know that?'

I shook my head, increasingly incensed.

'They could be filming you right now and you wouldn't even know. They pay us to keep the peace round here, so upstarts like you don't come along making mischief. Let's see your ID then.'

I'd left my license in the back pocket of my trousers, so it too had surely vanished into the washing machine.

'It's inside,' I replied, maintaining my composure. 'I'm telling you, I work here…'

'And what are we supposed to believe your job is?'

'I'm a painter.'

'Oh yeah right,' said the guy in the hat. 'You've no idea the number of "painters" we've met round here who say they've come about a job.'

'No, not that kind of painter! I paint canvases, copies of old artworks.'

'An artist, huh,' he said, bored, his hands on his waist. 'And you think that means you're gonna get the royal treatment?'

'Say, what have you got there?' asked the stringy one, pointing at the box of paints with his truncheon.

'It's my paintbox. The owner hired me to do a painting and I went out for materials. I'm waiting for them to let me in.'

'You don't say…' The stringy one grabbed the box from me, opened it, and showed his companion what was inside. The two burst out laughing. It was full of crayons, plasticine, marbles, toy cars…

'You're really asking for it, you are.'

'Come on, in you get,' said the older guy, as though leading a mule.

'Get rid of that junk, let the rubbish guys take it,' said the stringy policeman, and his companion threw my box towards a bin a few metres away on the pavement. He missed. It landed on a corner and the crunch of wood sounded like my own skull splitting open. I couldn't take it any more. As one of the cops was handcuffing me, I shoved him against the pickup and tried to make a run for it. I hadn't even managed to free my arms when the truncheon blows started raining down on my back and head. Thumps, kicks, taunts. They threw me limp into the back of the van with my hands cuffed behind my back.

'Here's one for you to look after, Socket. Just don't let him out until we say so,' the policeman with the hat said to a homeless man curled up on the floor of the pickup.

The vehicle set off. The homeless man greeted me with a nod, his eyes hooded. He smiled like he was welcoming me to a party – like he was about to offer me a beer so we could sit down for a chat. His gums were swollen, and his teeth were coated in a greenish paste. He was wrapped in a grimy blanket and a thick mop of grey hair hid half his face. He stank so much I had to turn my face into the wind to quell my nausea.

When we arrived at the police station, they locked us in the same cell, a tiny two-by-two metre square room with nothing but a bucket of water and a toilet, half covered over with a piece of cardboard. The walls had once been white, which made the dirt, rust and scratches even more noticeable.

'Poor old Socket, you'll have to share a room tonight,' the policeman in the hat told the homeless man.

We extended our wrists through the bars and they uncuffed us. The stringy policeman allowed himself the luxury of twisting my arms until I yowled in pain. I tumbled to the floor when he let me go, and there I stayed, still as a corpse whose eyes nobody had bothered to close.

'See?' said the guy in the hat, 'that's what you get for being uppity. Better shut up next time and do what you're told.'

'And you, you son of a bitch, do you never learn? We've told you a thousand times you can't go wandering round that neighbourhood. Jesus, Socket. How hard is it to stay downtown?'

'Thing is, I don't like living in a house, I prefer the open air,' the homeless man replied brightly. 'This is my kingdom – the whole mountain's mine, the Colomos forest, the horses, the ducks – '

'Damn you, Socket, you're wrong in the head, you are. There's plenty of fresh air down in Zapopan, you stay there. Anyway, cough up. What have you got for me?'

'Only enough for the fee, comandante.' He straightened up and took a ball of newspaper out of his jacket, which he handed over to the police.

'Alright then, nighty night. I'll get you some beans or something later.'

I was watching the old homeless man, his strange smile and cheerful air. He'd lain down on the floor of the cell, legs crossed, head propped up against the base of the wall. He looked like he was lying on a beach.

Then he plucked a joint rolled from a trolleybus ticket out of the hem of his trousers and lit it without a second thought. The smell of weed spread through the cell, but nobody seemed to notice. He took a couple of puffs and then reached over to me.

'Here, have a smoke,' he said. I was still pretty dazed. 'It'll do you good. Go on, take it.'

He brought the joint right to my face and stuck it in my mouth with two dirty fingers. When I could move again, I held the stub myself.

I used to smoke sometimes with friends, with Felipe and the other painters in the studio, though in recent months I'd had neither the money nor the urge. Right then, though, exhausted and bashed about as I was, a bit of weed was like manna from heaven. It wasn't long before I felt lighter, like I was peeling away from the pain. Socket's face, placid and squint-eyed, made me laugh.

It was after dark when I woke up desperately thirsty. Between us we chugged down half a bucket of water; at once my stomach was seized by a primal hunger. Socket took out a packet of Japanese peanuts which we both devoured. Later, the flabby policeman, no longer wearing his hat, brought us a couple of bean burritos wrapped in tin foil and turned out the lights. Socket pulled off a piece and told me to eat the rest. I tried to refuse, but he said, 'My stomach's literally this big,' and touched his four fingers to his thumb as though holding a little ball. We stretched out on the floor of the cell and I fell into a deep sleep.

We both woke wrapped in the dirty blanket. A new policeman rattled the bars and yelled: 'Alright, you bastards, run along home!'

I got up as best I could. There wasn't a single part of my body that didn't hurt. I was limping, frozen stiff, and I could taste blood in my mouth. Outside, I recognised neither the street nor the neighbourhood, though I knew we were a long way from where we'd been picked up.

Socket asked where I was headed but I could only shrug my shoulders. I started to hobble towards a crossing I could make out a couple of blocks up ahead. Apparently stronger than I was, the wiry old fellow tucked his shoulder under my armpit so I could lean on him. He gave me a half turn and started taking me in the opposite direction; I let him lead me for a few streets. When I felt a bit less numb, I walked by myself. I recognised the area. He was taking me back to Horacio's house.

'No, listen, I don't want to go back there,' I protested. 'There's no way to get in, and if the police see me again while I'm waiting for somebody to come out, they'll lock me up for good this time.'

'Hang on, man, follow me.'

So I did, and we soon came to the entrance with the lions.

'This door has a little wire here…'

He crouched down at the foot of the sheet metal door and stuck his fingers under the bottom. He tugged the wire and the door swung open.

'There we are… See? I'm telling you, this is my kingdom!'

He left, smiling, without saying goodbye, the fringes of his blanket dragging along the ground.

4.

I crossed the empty lot like a fugitive, terrified of being spotted by the security cameras I imagined hidden in the undergrowth. I stepped carefully, glancing in all directions, but I didn't see or hear a thing, not even as I slipped my hand through the broken window to open the little metal door. The garden was silent, deserted. The staff weren't up yet. It was so easy to break in. Anyone could enter the house and steal objects worth millions. But who would know that there was a wire, an empty lot, a shattered pane?

Horacio's father's remains were safe in the vault, but everything else was just strewn around. Sure, the precious antiques that decorated the house would be tough for a thief to carry away in his arms, but it still puzzled me that they should be so exposed.

Then I thought of *La Morisca* and the paradox finally dawned on me. It was as if part of my mind saw what was happening before the rest of me did. My knees buckled, I froze halfway down the stairs, and a second later realised that neither I nor anyone else could steal *La Morisca* for the very same reason that the painting was impossible to forge: the chapel was a stone mass closed in on all six sides, and the only door was less than sixty centimetres across.

I rushed to the corner where ferns were sprouting from cracks between the stones, in order to confirm what was already obvious. Looking up, I wondered how the hell they'd ever got the panel all the way up there, not to mention the altarpiece that supported it. Only then did I grasp what Horacio had told me about the house having been built to protect the painting.

I paced around the terrace, peering up to the top of the wall and imagining the house under construction, the painting and altarpiece set down in the middle of the stark, dusty lot, draped in sheets and tarps, while the builders raised the walls around them, the centring, the roof. I imagined the architect Luis Barragán chuckling at the solution, so simple and yet so elegant.

What an idiot I was. Why hadn't I realised it sooner? That there was no way I could move the panel into the chapel, and that it was equally impossible to remove the painting so I could work on the forgery from the studio – why hadn't Horacio mentioned this minor inconvenience? My spirits plummeted. I'd better get used to the thought of disappearing. I never cashed the cheque; officially, nothing had happened here. Horacio could hardly complain. Let him beg the Miracolo Torino to work his magic – or else tear down the entire house to get the thing out.

I leaned against the mossy wall and looked around. The tranquillity of the house was infuriating. The tips of the climbers trailed gently on the steaming surface of the pool as the yellow light of the morning sun spilled into the treetops. The birds were starting up their clamour, but the oppressive silence inside me was heavier than all the stones piled up behind my back.

I dragged my feet toward the studio, the damp from the cell still rusting my joints. I was in no rush to be back out on the streets. I needed to rest. I longed to fall into bed, but I reeked of my own sweat mixed with the stench of Socket's piss-stained blanket, so I went straight to the bathroom, flung my dirty clothes into a corner and turned the water on. I felt a rush of pleasure as the dense, hot stream struck my back. The boiler was permanently on; in rich people's houses, everything works the way it's supposed to. I closed my eyes and let the water melt my bones. I opened a box of fragrant soap and scrubbed myself down three or four times over. Once clean, I pulled on a t-shirt and a pair of boxers from the stack of clothes that Tona had left on the chair, slipped between the sheets and fell asleep at once.

It was almost entirely dark when I woke, and for a moment I had no idea where I was. Then I recognised the bedroom and remembered what had happened: the eviction, the prison cell, the impossibility of forging the painting. I had nowhere to go. I sat on the edge of the bed and started trying to figure out how to extricate myself from this mess, but everything that came to mind was far-fetched or ridiculous – like appealing to Señora Chang, who surely thought I'd stolen her triptych. I felt sluggish, dazed. I went to the bathroom, lowered my head to the tap and drank about a litre of water in one go. I hadn't eaten in two days and my stomach ached as if it contained a handful of buckshot. I looked pale.

I got dressed and went to the kitchen. The bottle-green shutters were closed over the counter that looked out onto the terrace. The creak of the swinging door echoed through the house, but the servants seemed to be out – a relief, as far as I was concerned. I could eat undisturbed and then leave without having to explain myself. At most, I'd write Horacio a note and leave him to sort things out as best he could. I had quite enough to worry about already.

The kitchen – stove in the middle, marble counter-tops, wooden cabinets on all sides – looked like the set of a photo shoot for an interior design magazine. A leaded glass lampshade cast a soft glow onto a brimming fruit bowl, ready to be painted into a still life. My stomach growled; I was desperate to eat something. I opened the fridge and found countless cheeses, meats, vegetables and jars of unfamiliar foods. Without a second thought, I wolfed down a cocktail sausage and took a great gulp of orange juice right from the carton. I grabbed a salami as long as my arm, a hunk of holey cheese, an avocado and anything else that looked like it could go in a sandwich. I found a bread basket full of fresh rolls on the counter. Splitting three down the middle, I spread them with mustard and mayonnaise, stuffed them with everything I'd taken out and scarfed the first one so fast I barely tasted it.

The house was utterly still. The only noise came from the refrigerator, which soon went quiet as well. The silence overwhelmed me: it forced me to think, and thinking was the last thing I wanted to do just then. All the problems jostled around in my mind, elbowing each other in attempts to distinguish themselves and get solved. I decided to start with the note I'd leave for Horacio. I found a little notepad and a pen nearby. What would I reproach him for first? The loss of my apartment, or the fact that he'd hired me to forge the piece without bothering to mention that it was impossible, that it was literally walled in with stone and clay? Maybe I should just write out my resignation and have done with it.

But I was reluctant to quit. It was so nice being there, safe and sound. A clean bed, a fridge full of food. All the things I could paint in a studio like that. Everything I'd ever wanted was there – and yet I couldn't have it, because there was no way to forge the painting, impounded as it was within those stone walls. Unless… unless I copied it from memory. On the notepad in front of me, I sketched the outlines of what I could recall, the fundamentals of the painting: the woman's features, the six pillars in the background, the perspective, the proportions of each object. If I could memorise the details, brushstroke by brushstroke, I might be able to eke it out in my head and then recreate it in the forgery. It sounded insane. I took a box of matches and opened the chapel door. The darkness exhaled its cavernous breath, but I felt more and more exhilarated by the idea of carrying out this ludicrous plan. I strode purposefully inside and lit a candle to compare my crude sketch with the work itself. There it was. The essence of the painting came through in the outline I had penned. Having seen the piece only once, I'd managed to memorise the most important parts largely without effort. I could do it. I could copy the painting from memory. Or at least I could try.

Back in the studio, I was feverish with excitement. I itched for daybreak. I started rummaging through the piles of junk in search of a pencil and paper when I came across an old-looking record player. The device was intact; only the acrylic surface was fractured. A box of LPs sat beside it. I hauled it all into the little living area and hooked up the cables and speakers. It worked perfectly. I listened to an album by the Hermanas Aguilera as I furiously churned out sketch after sketch of the painting. Then I started drawing faces and landscapes I'd seen over the years. I conjured meticulous details from memory: a rip in the upholstery of a sofa, the number of tiles in a mosaic on a kitchen floor, the border of a piece of lattice work. As a student, I became quite notorious for my near-photographic memory, but I'd never given it much thought; it was just something I could do to show off. Until then I'd never imagined how useful it could be.

By dawn, the notepad was full of sketches and pencil shavings were scattered around my feet. I felt a wave of clean, contented exhaustion that sent me straight back to bed. I woke mid-morning, ready to get to work.

El Gordo was mowing the lawn; Tona pottered in the kitchen. She smirked as I approached and filled a pitcher with coffee.

'Where have you been hiding then? I thought you weren't coming back. What did we do to scare him off, I asked myself, there was only that one little hiccup, that accident – nothing that can't be fixed, you'll see, as soon as my Horacio comes home.'

'Everything's fine, don't worry. I was just sorting a few things out before I get started,' I said solemnly.

'Sit yourself down and have some breakfast. When you're finished El Gordo will take you to buy whatever you need.'

She placed a basket of bread on the table, followed a few minutes later by an enormous plate of enmoladas drenched in fresh cheese and sour cream.

As I ate, I heard a parrot cawing 'Gordo! Gordo!' and El Gordo appeared on the terrace with a red macaw perched on his forearm. He was smiling. Tona set a platter of fruit on the counter. 'That's for your girlfriend,' she said to him.

'Girlfriend,' he echoed in a thick voice, the voice of a deaf man.

El Gordo raised a cube of fruit to the bird's beak. The parrot gulped it down and shifted its enormous leadwort blue wings, swaying happily on the arm of the man who was feeding it. It cast me an occasional wary glance. Next to El Gordo, it seemed sharp-witted and perceptive, as if it were more attuned to reality than he was.

'Now get that thing out of here. It makes me nervous. And all it does is make a mess,' Tona teased as she peeled the papery shells off some tomatillos.

'Girlfriend,' El Gordo murmured again, turning away.

'Oh, and once you're done, you can take our guest to buy some things for his work. Here...'

She set the manila envelope of bills onto the counter, the same one that Horacio had left on his departure. El Gordo stuffed the envelope into his shirt and walked away with both the macaw and the fruit platter.

I set my cutlery onto the plate and wiped the sauce from my mouth with a starched cloth napkin. I'd have to start with a scale drawing. Then I'd expand it to full size, compare the two and take notes. I needed to clean and prepare the panel, mix the paints, the tempera... *How long did it take Mabuse to do it?* I wondered. But that was a different time.

We headed out. El Gordo followed me through the empty lot, four or five steps behind. I was thinking we'd hail a taxi on the main avenue, but before I knew it he'd overtaken me and got into the truck parked next to the pile of sand. It was a pickup, like mine, but much older and more beaten up. He started the ignition and put his foot down a couple of times to warm up the engine. I was still standing by the passenger window. How on earth is this guy supposed to be able to drive when his eyes don't even focus, I wondered. The engine was ready. I was going to say it would be better if I took the wheel, but in the end I let him get on with it. I figured I could always ask him to switch. To my surprise, El Gordo turned out to be a natural.

I asked him to take me to the centre of town, and then to a shop in Tlaquepaque where I always bought the raw pigments to prepare my paints. But before we got downtown he parked in a little street in the Santa Tere neighbourhood. I thought he must have to sort out some errand of his own, so I set about leafing through an old newspaper while I waited for him. When he saw I wasn't getting out, he came round and opened the door for me; I put the newspaper down and followed him.

El Gordo rang the bell of one of those single-story houses with smooth façades and a window ledge crowded with ceramic figurines that stared at us as we waited in the glare. On the pavement there was nothing but a stumpy bitter orange tree. All the pavements in Santa Tere are full of those dirty-leaved trees, and as you walk you've got to duck to avoid ending up with their thorns buried in your scalp.

An older man, very tall and thin, opened the door. When he saw El Gordo he stepped to one side to let us in. Behind him you could just make out a living room and beyond it a patio. From one of the rooms came a voice, somehow both hoarse and piercing:

'Who is it?'

'It's them, Mother,' replied the thin man.

'Who?'

'Just a moment, please,' the thin man said to me, and disappeared into the house.

'It's him. The man the maestro sent.' He was practically shouting at his mother, as though the old lady was half-deaf.

'Tell him to wait for me, I'm coming.'

I didn't have the faintest idea what we were doing there, nor who these people were. The house's gloomy atmosphere was beginning to freak me out. The man returned holding an orange and gave it to El Gordo, who looked thrilled and hunched over at once to peel it.

'Melesio Ramírez, at your service.' He held his hand out to me.

'Thank you, I'm José Federico Burgos.'

'A pleasure, Señor Burgos. The maestro paid a visit to

74

tell us you would be coming.'

'I'm sorry, Señor Ramírez, but I'm not here on behalf of any maestro. Are you sure you're not confusing me with somebody else?'

'The maestro wants to train you and has asked that you be assessed first. There is no confusion.'

'But I don't know anything about that. Who is this maestro you keep mentioning?'

'The maestro no longer belongs to this world. Perhaps our dear Horacio mentioned him to you.'

The woman emerged from the bedroom in slippers and a nightgown, her white hair dishevelled, leaning on a Zimmer frame that crunched like bones with every step. She slowly crossed the living room in the direction of the patio. She tried to make it down the steps and out, but couldn't seem to bend her knees.

'Allow me,' said the man, bowing with theatrical solemnity, and went to help his mother.

El Gordo was absorbed in eating his orange; there was no point in making conversation. Melesio called me from the door to the patio. He had sat the woman down in a wicker chair with a large circular backrest, like a throne. The chair stood at the foot of an enormous guava tree whose branches were hung with countless objects: little jars, dolls, gifts wrapped in faded cellophane, ribbons, necklaces, banknotes secured with pins. The hair stood up on the back of my neck. This could only be some sort of witchcraft, and I wanted out of there, but Melesio was looming over me from behind, impeding my retreat.

The woman sat still in her chair. Her eyes were full of cataracts and seemed to be staring at a point somewhere above my shoulder. She moved her dry, bony hands as if stroking some invisible animal on her lap.

'Ask me your question.' Her voice was much fuller and deeper now.

75

'What question?' I asked, disconcerted. I thought perhaps I was supposed to ask her about my future, or beg for some advice, but nothing came to mind. I stood there like a statue, my hands grasped in front of me, fingers interlaced.

'You are you...?'

'Excuse me?' I asked, not understanding.

'The question is, you are you?' she repeated by way of response. 'If you are you, then you will seal the destiny of those who must be released. He who finds the door also finds the key.'

She was silent. I looked to one side, then the other, but nothing happened. The wind gusted and shadows walked over the ground without any of us noticing.

'Now leave your offering,' she added.

I looked at the tree and understood I was supposed to hang something of mine there, or pin a banknote up. I rummaged in my pockets but all I had with me were my keys and the end of a pencil I'd been drawing with. El Gordo had the envelope full of money, so I left the pencil stub. I wrapped it in a dirty piece of string I found discarded on the floor and tied it to one of the less crowded branches. When I turned around again, the old lady was asleep, her head resting on the back of the chair and her mouth half-open. Melesio came over and indicated that I should follow him to the back of the patio where there was an even older structure, high-ceilinged and made of adobe.

As soon as he opened the door, my nose recognised the damp freshness of the minerals stored there: it was the smell of a paint shop. Which is what the little room seemed to be. Melesio tugged the string dangling from a bleary lightbulb above the counter and put on a canvas apron stained with different colours. He began taking out containers and putting them on the counter. He still used cones made out of old newspaper.

Without a word from me, he began measuring out a bit of this and a bit of that. The basic colours: titanium white, ochre, brick red. I let him get on with it.

'The maestro said you work for a very important company and that we should provide you with all the materials you need. If you find you're missing something, all you have to do is send El Gordo to pick it up.'

I thanked him. The whole 'maestro' thing was making my skin crawl, so I tried to distract myself looking at the glass cabinets full of little eyes for sculptures, agate stones, tiny charms shaped like the hands of saints and old brand products you couldn't find in regular hardware stores any more. I began to feel like a child in a sweet shop.

Melesio put the containers away under the counter and pulled out another series of rectangular tins, their tops sliced open diagonally. These were the rarer pigments. Indigo, vermillion, sienna, malachite, vine black, Cyprus umber, as well as saffron and cochineal. I was dying to get my hands inside the boxes, touch the colours, feel the clumps crumble between my fingers.

'How much of these will you be needing...'

'Two hundred grams of each, if you'd be so kind.'

Melesio pouted slightly. Perhaps I was pushing it, and he was sorry to part with so large a part of his treasure trove.

'Is this realgar powder?'

'It is. Arsenic sulphide. Extremely poisonous. They stopped making it more than forty years ago, I'm surprised you recognised it.'

'A long time ago, when I was learning to paint, we'd use it to give faces a final touch, to bring complexions to life. It gives skin a tone that's impossible to achieve with any other pigment.'

The man didn't look up from his process of weighing and measuring colours on the scales.

'I'm going to need lavender and poppy seed oils. Do you know where I can get them?'

'I've got lavender and linseed, but there's only a hundred millilitres of poppy seed left. On López Cotilla Street there's a pharmacy I know has it. If you tell the owner I sent you, you might convince him to sell you some. At an exorbitant price, mind you.'

He had folded the newspaper cones of pigment closed and put them in a sack with the tins of oil. In the shop he also had paintbrushes, spatulas and other things, but I didn't want to abuse his generosity any further – I could buy that sort of stuff in Casa Serra or anywhere else. All the rare items I'd found there were more than enough for now.

As I crossed the patio back towards the house we passed the guava tree again, but the old lady was gone. Don Melesio gave the sack to El Gordo. I asked the man to say goodbye to his mother for me. He nodded and went to open the door. We left, got into the pickup and El Gordo started the ignition. I felt light, satisfied.

'I can't believe the things that man has in his shop! I've been looking for realgar powder for years,' I said to El Gordo, excited, not expecting him to respond. 'Now the hard part will be preparing all the paints. I'll have to grind and grind and grind them until the clumps completely disappear… Ah, we're heading for the centre, if you don't mind! There's loads of stuff we still need. The good thing is we've already got poppy seed oil. I think this'll be enough. Listen… actually, I don't know why I'm even asking you, but that whole thing about the 'maestro' is really weird, who were they talking about?'

We stopped at a traffic light. El Gordo managed to get his wandering eyes to focus for a second on my face. He smiled.

We spent the better part of the day doing the rounds from shop to shop, buying charcoal, manila paper, limewash, glue, spatulas, a pestle and mortar, glass, paintbrushes and palettes, turpentine, empty jars, anything that occurred to me I might need. We'd go into a shop, the person on duty would bring me whatever I asked, and El Gordo would pull the envelope of money out of his overalls to pay. After the third or fourth shop, El Gordo preferred to entrust me with the envelope and wait, double parked, outside.

When I saw just how much money there was, it occurred to me that I could buy a camera. How had I not thought of that before! With a camera I could take photos of all the painting's details. I asked El Gordo to take me to Plaza Patria. It must have been five o'clock by then and we were starving, so before anything else we went to have lunch at a place in the centre where they serve enormous portions and two litre jugs of juice. El Gordo's eyes lit up at a photo on the menu of a gigantic fruit cocktail, enough to feed an army, with whipped cream, granola, chocolate syrup and a cherry on top. He also ordered a jug of guava juice and waffles. I ordered an escalope, but the dish came with Russian salad, sweet-corn, beans, rice, salad, chips and steamed vegetables. To drink I ordered a beer, also large.

I had never seen anyone eat with such gusto as El Gordo tackling his family-sized fruit cocktail. We ate until we couldn't. When it came to paying, I realised the place was so cheap it was ridiculous to have chosen to eat there, given all the money we had on us.

We arrived at the plaza and I asked El Gordo to wait for me in the parking lot. In addition to the camera I'd need some clothes. I wandered the aisles a couple of times without finding anything I'd consider wearing. I wasn't used to shopping in places like that – the outfits they'd dressed the mannequins in seemed too extravagant. I was soon fed up, though I hadn't bought a single thing. In the end I went to Kodak and asked them to sell me the best automatic camera they had. The most expensive. I also bought four films, batteries, and a couple of replacement flashes. Before leaving the car park I spotted a shop with vinyl on offer – and I was off, buying everything that took my fancy.

I got into the pickup laden with bags. El Gordo started the engine and put it in reverse. A man stopped the traffic so we could back out, whistling and waving with a red flannel. I recognised him. It was Socket. My heart leapt as though I'd met an old friend. If it hadn't been for him, I wouldn't have survived that night. I called to him through the open window, said hi and gave him a fifty-peso note.

'I've got no change right now, sir, thank you kindly,' he apologised, and tried to give me back the banknote.

'No, no, Socket, it's me, from the other day, in the cell, remember?'

'How could I forget, after you hugged me all night long,' he laughed, tucking the bill into his pocket. 'Hey, that whole thing with your box was really rough. I asked the guys in the trailer, they're gonna look for the pieces. You never know, maybe they'll find them.'

'Seriously? Thanks so much, man, I'd be really grateful.'

'I'm not promising anything, mind… but we'll see. Are all those records yours?'

'I suppose they are, yeah…'

'Nice, I'll look forward to my invite to come over and listen to music.'

'For sure, one of these days.'

I said it in all sincerity. I would have liked to take Socket out and save him like he'd saved me, but listening to music together, however you looked at it, seemed more or less impossible.

Socket went back to the street to hold up the traffic, waving his red flannel.

5.

We headed back to the house. El Gordo left the bags at the entrance to the studio and went to see his macaw, which was squawking insistently at the back of the garden. It was too late to take the photos – there was barely any light left – so I used the time to put away all the materials we'd just bought.

I'd planned to make a life-size sketch and mark it up with notes on colour, deterioration and glazes, so I was going to need a huge piece of paper. With this in mind, I'd bought myself several sheets of manila paper, and I set about sticking them together with masking tape until they were the size of the panel. I worked quietly on the floor of the studio, listening to one of the new records by Ella Fitzgerald. Don Lalo's friends had often spoken about her music, but I hadn't had the opportunity to hear it before. Now I listened from start to finish a number of times until I could match the songs with the titles on the sleeve. I rolled up the giant sheet of paper and propped it in a corner. It was really good to be there.

It had been a long and productive day and I was knackered. After our enormous lunch, I wasn't hungry, but I did fancy an ice-cold beer before bed. I waited until

Tona had gone up to her room so I could raid the fridge, then took the last two cans in a six pack, along with a piece of cheese.

As I left, I noticed a telephone mounted on the wall behind the swing door. The handset was dangling upside down from its cable. I held it to my ear and heard an electric hum, but no dialling tone. I pushed the switch hook a couple of times, but nothing, just that continuous buzz. Then something rustled on the other end of the line. Someone breathing.

'Tona…? Can you hear me? Tona… Hello…?' It was a woman's voice. A thick, slightly gravelly voice. 'Tona, answer me, for god's sake, it's urgent!'

'Hello? Señora, I can hear you. Tona isn't here. I think she's gone to bed.'

'Who's speaking?'

'I'm… a painter, I'm doing some work here in the house. I saw the phone off the hook, heard you calling and answered. Would you like me to get Señora Tona for you? She must be in her room.'

'Oh, no no, I won't trouble you. Painter, you said?'

'Yes, Señora. A copyist.'

'Are you a friend of my son's?'

'Yes. Well – Horacio is your son?'

'Of course. Didn't he tell you?'

'No, no he didn't tell me about you, but in truth we don't know each other very well, he only recently hired me to help him with a piece of work. You said you needed something urgently, are you sure you don't want me to call Señora Tona? I'm sure she'll be awake, it's still early – assuming she hasn't gone out, that is.'

'Oh, I'm sorry to bother you, it's just I'm a bit under the weather. She said she'd bring me some medicine but you know how forgetful servants can be.'

'Are you alright? You don't need me to call a doctor?'

'No, no, I'm fine, don't worry. It's really nothing serious at all.'

'Well, if you let me know what medicine you need, I'll happily bring it to you. The only thing is it's a bit late and I don't know where El Gordo keeps the car keys.'

'You're very kind. But I wouldn't trouble you with such a thing.'

'It's no trouble, truly. If you tell me your address, I'll bring you the medicine right away.'

'But I'm here, in the house. Where else would I be?'

'Ahhh! I'm sorry, I didn't know. Well in that case there's no question, just tell me what you need.'

'Oh, I do hate to put you out. If only I could go myself. The medicine should be in one of the kitchen drawers. It's a glass dropper bottle with a blue label that says Xanax.'

'Xan…' I stretched the cord as far as it would go, so I could check the drawers. 'Here it is! Xanax. I suppose you'll need a glass of water…'

'I have one here, thank you. Mine's the last door down the hall, on the left.' She hung up.

I glanced over my shoulder. I didn't know what to do with the handset, whether to leave it as it was or put it back in its place. I decided to leave it exactly as Tona had done.

I went to the last door at the end of the corridor. I called out, but nobody answered. I thought Horacio's mother might be in bed, so I opened the door very slowly and called again. The air was still, pregnant with a thick sweet perfume, like vanilla. The light from the hallway meant I couldn't see inside. The carpet muffled the noise so well the effect was almost violent. I asked again, more loudly, if I could come in, but nobody answered. Perhaps she simply didn't want to be seen. There was a large eagle claw-foot table in the middle of the room. I went over and left the bottle there, then turned on my heel and strode across the room as though the silence were pursuing me.

The next morning, I took enough photographs of *La Morisca* to fill my four rolls of film. I shot the panel from every possible angle, with every kind of light I could improvise, considering there was no electricity inside the chapel. An aluminium stepladder I'd found leaning against a tree served as a scaffold, allowing me to capture the details near the top. I felt relaxed and content. I'd stayed in bed until nine or ten, when there was decent lighting, then had a shower and eaten breakfast. Once I'd finished with the photos, I asked El Gordo to drive me to the plaza again so I could get them developed.

An hour later I picked up four yellow envelopes full of photos and opened them there and then, on the countertop in the photo lab. My enthusiasm instantly evaporated. Not a single photo had come out right. The close-ups were blurry; the ones from afar were either too dark or blanched with light. It was a complete disaster. At most I could save maybe one or two photos from each envelope, but they'd only be useful for capturing the general shape of things. You couldn't make out any brushstrokes or details, the colours were too dark and the painting's proportions had been distorted by the lens.

I felt like throwing the bag of photos in the bin or smashing the counter with my fist, but I contained myself and went back out into the car park. El Gordo started the pickup and I waited as he negotiated a way out. As he turned towards one of the exits to the tunnel, I saw Socket running over.

'How's it going, bro? So good to see you. Hey, can you lend me a hundred pesos? It's important.'

'Come on, man, I gave you fifty yesterday!'

'I'm saving up though.'

'You really are a scrounger, aren't you. Here.' I gave him the change from the photos.

'Guess that's better than nothing. Hey, what's that?'

'Oh, just some photos, but they didn't come out right.'

'Can I see them?'

'They're of the painting I'm going to copy, but they're all really blurry.'

'You're copying a painting? Ha.'

'What's funny about that?'

'Just that painters copy what they see, and you want to copy a copy. Isn't that kind of pointless?'

'Well, if it means getting paid…'

'Ah, well, you got me there. I don't need you down here taking all my business, do I?'

'You joke, but one of these days I'll end up directing traffic just like you.'

'Anytime, I'll get you a foot in the door. Can you do this?' He rolled the tip of his tongue between his lips and let out an intermittent whistle. We laughed. 'So, what, you're going to chuck them away?' He pointed to the photos. 'Because if you're going to throw them out, I'll take them off your hands.'

'Nah, what would I give them to you for? I'm sure I'll get some use out of them.'

'Fine, just one then. For my art collection.'

'Go on then, here, have this one.'

El Gordo pulled the pickup around and I got in. In the rear view mirror I saw Socket waving goodbye with the photo. He ran down the edge of the pavement like a scrap of newspaper swept along by the wind.

I was going to have to hurry. Just preparing the oils was a laborious and lengthy task, though if I was honest playing the alchemist was almost my favourite part of the process – mixing this and that, doing experiments.

First I had to heat the linseed oil in a bain-marie. There was a kitchenette full of junk at the back of the studio. I shifted some boxes to clear space on the hob and checked there was gas – all I had to do was open a valve. I pinched a couple of old saucepans from the kitchen and set them on the hob. To prepare the Dammar glaze I would need a woman's stocking to use as a filter. My only option was to ask Tona to lend me one of hers, then deal with two or three days of her winding me up with comments like 'if you wanted a pair of my stockings so badly, you only had to ask, darling' and 'so you're the type who likes to keep souvenirs then, are you?' In the end even I found it funny. I had to crush the nuggets of resin and empty them into the stocking inside a bottle of turpentine to filter out residues that would otherwise end up in the paint. The studio started to fill with that familiar resin-smell of workshops and galleries.

The final step was the trickiest: mixing the earth pigments with the binding agent, judging the proportions by eye and tempering the mixture with a spatula on a piece of marble like it was chocolate. Eventually I decanted the prepared paint into a clean aluminium tube that was open at the bottom. Once it was almost full, I flattened it out like toothpaste, folded it over at the end and sealed it with pliers.

I spent whole days engrossed in this process, grinding pigments and mixing ingredients. The turpentine fumes plunged me into a lucid stupor from which I only emerged to change the record or go to the toilet. The universe seemed to fill with a sea of cobalt blue or vermillion red and nothing else. I would have forgotten to eat and even drink if it hadn't been for El Gordo bringing in a tray every few hours. He'd approach quietly, his eyes wandering, and nose curiously through everything I was doing.

'Do you want to give it a go?' I asked, and without waiting for an answer I put the stone pestle in his hand and showed him how to move his wrist to grind out the lumps. At first he held it clumsily, uncertainly, like a baby smashing at pureed food, but I let him carry on and he began to figure it out before long. I corrected him a couple of times and that was enough for him to master the technique. And so the hours went by, until we heard the thundering of Tona's hysterical voice as she called him from across the garden. Terrified, El Gordo put down the pestle, wiped his hands on his overalls and heeded his sister's call. It wasn't easy to convince her that she should let him help me for a while each afternoon, but when I insisted, arguing that Horacio's priority was for the painting to be finished on time, she had no choice but to accept.

Once I'd finished mixing the colours, I finally had to stop putting off the main task at hand and tackle *La Morisca* once and for all. A kind of panic had prevented me from starting. Perhaps it was the other painting hidden underneath the tarpaulin, like a sacrificial lamb, its eyes covered to shield it from the spectre of death. But one night – one of the many nights I couldn't sleep, frustrated and worried about how little time I had left – I finally took the plunge. I grabbed a wire brush and a spray bottle full of turpentine, ripped the tarpaulin off in a single tug, doused *David the Shepherd* in solvent and, galvanised by self-loathing, started to scrub.

PART TWO

PART TWO

I hear birds twittering as they wake. Some tree must be teeming with them, beset by birds and their noise. Beyond them, far in the distance, I can hear the wail of an approaching siren. It comes round the bend in the road and stops as it reaches me.

Someone pries my eyelids open and shines a torch into each pupil. It's a woman. She speaks to me. She asks if I can hear her, asks my name. 'My name is José Federico Burgos, I fell from that wall over there, I've hurt my right hand, help me.' She asks again if I can hear her, and I realise the words are stuck in my mouth. 'My hand's in a bad way, fix it, don't amputate it. Please don't cut it off, I'm begging you. I'm a painter, please don't amputate my hand.' I try desperately to explain, but my tongue is knotted, like when you're paralysed in your sleep and try to scream but your voice never leaves your throat.

'Wake up!' She shakes my head back and forth. 'Try to open your eyes. Look over here! Can you hear me?'

'He's about to have a seizure,' says another voice, a young man's. 'Give me fifty grams of phenytoin.'

A seizure? But I can't feel anything. Are they talking about me? I feel an electric current crackle through me from head to toe, as if I'd touched an exposed wire. Right, that must be it. How odd – it feels like someone is tickling my brain. An unbearable tickle that erases everything I am and plunges me into total silence. I take a deep dive into the silent pool and sink there, floating in the darkness.

I don't know how much time has passed, but somehow I'm sure it's long enough for the doctors to have fixed my broken body. I know I'm safe. I rise like a bubble to the surface of sleep. I'm so light that I rise and rise, effortlessly ascending through the clear water of a glimmering sea.

I break through the surface, but my eyes are still closed. I decide to stay there, absorbing everything I can before anyone notices I'm awake. Human murmurs, a baby's cry, the clicking of heels, all reverberating against the floor of a cavernous dome, the echo of a church or colonial building.

The air smells of fresh bandages. The stench of blood and waste tries to conceal itself, but antiseptics are too shoddy a garment, too worn, nauseatingly eager to hide the affliction of sick flesh. A cool breeze wafts in from the side. Trees shifting in the wind. The drone of a bus engine on the street.

I'm in a high-ceilinged wing with limewashed walls. A scrap of sky shines through one of the barred windows near the ceiling. There must be about twenty beds. The compartments are divided with curtains that barely reach head height, and they're no wider than half a bed across. I immediately glance at my hand to make sure it's still there. It is, but it's strung up in a crazy contraption of gauze straps and poles, like a Bedouin tent. I don't dare move it.

On the other side of me, a woman is praying. A nun in a white habit clutching a rosary. She's pressing her eyes shut and moving her lips. As I decipher a murmured *now and in the hour of our death, amen,* I close my eyes again, but I'm too slow, and she notices.

'Holy Mary, Mother of God! I think the young man has woken up.'

I try hard to look like I'm still asleep, but my eyes strain against my lids as if spring-operated and my bladder is suddenly fit to explode. The praying nun now stands at the foot of my bed, accompanied by a squat woman in a brown habit and thick bifocals.

'Now just where do you think you're going?' the Mother Superior demands when she sees me struggling to get up.

'I need to use the bathroom.'

'Number one or number two?'

'I have to urinate,' I answer, intensely embarrassed.

'There's the bedpan. You're not going anywhere until the doctor says so. He won't be long; he starts his rounds at ten. Give him a hand, won't you, dear?'

The nun turns and walks away. Her tunic swells in the air, like the skirts of little girls spinning each other around in the playground.

The nun in the white habit takes the metal receptacle and slips her hands under the sheet. I want to stop her, but my other hand is hooked up to the IV and all I manage to do is tangle the cables in the cloth.

'Tsk, tsk! Keep that hand down or the needle will clog and they'll have to jab you all over again.'

She gingerly picks up my flaccid member, which aches with the need to relieve itself. I flinch at her touch, then flinch again at the cold metal against my thighs. The urine warms it as my muscles relax. I must be blushing. I find it easiest to look up. There's a cross made of sticks above the bed and a little card taped to the wall: unknown/orthopaedics/dr emmanuel hernández, it says in marker pen.

'Is this the Hospital de Belén?'

'That's right. Have you been here before?'

I shake my head. 'Just in passing. I came to paint some watercolours in the cemetery once.'

'Ah, you're a painter!'

I nod half-heartedly as she lifts the sheet and removes the metal pan, her hands trembling.

'There's a painter who sometimes comes to work here. He's very kind. I think you should speak to him, maybe he can help you. I could tell him to stop by for a chat. He really is a lovely man, you'll see. Besides, Father Solís has instructed me to pray for you and help you find your way again. I think this could be a good start, don't you?'

I stare at her, my forehead creasing with confusion. I don't understand a thing.

'Don't you want to return to God? He gave his life for us, after all. Father Solís told me to call him as soon as you were ready to confess. Would you like me to call him?'

'Confess?' I repeat with a deepening frown, shaking my head.

'You must realise how lucky you are, Señor... I'm sorry, what was your name?'

'Burgos.'

'Jesus saved you, Señor Burgos. There's a reason why you're still in this world. It's a real miracle. Sometimes, despair makes us commit what may seem like unforgivable sins, but God is merciful: slow to anger and full of loving kindness.'

I don't know what I have to do to shut her up. I feel dizzy. I'm about to bark at her to leave me alone, that I'm an atheist, a communist, I'm Satan himself. But I hold back.

'Let me confess something to you, Señor Burgos.' She looks into my eyes, leans closer, and says in a tiny, fragile voice: 'I tried it too. I was desperate. I couldn't think of any other way. All I wanted was to stop living, deliver my soul to God and let him do his will. I cut myself here and here' – she shows me the scars on her wrists and I start to grasp what this sermon is all about. 'But God in his goodness wanted me to be found alive and I was saved. I realised that I could deliver my soul to Jesus without needing to die, because death is a terrible thing and I…'

She's weeping. The nun lets out a sob as harsh and sudden as a guffaw. She wipes her eyes with the sleeves of her habit. I feel incredibly awkward; I don't know how to comfort her. I'd have to explain that I didn't want to kill myself, that I jumped off the wall to flee the house and save my hand. But I can't.

'Forgive me, Señor Burgos. I shouldn't be so weak. I'm the one who's supposed to be helping you, and now look what's happened…'

I smile. She sniffles and smiles back.

'Will you let me help? Will you let me talk to the painter who comes to work on the murals?'

I nod. She takes my left hand with great care and I look into her eyes, swollen from tears but shining with relief.

'Thank you. Now then, I should be off. The doctor will be in soon.'

She walks away with her shoulders hunched and the metal pan still warm in her hands. Her disgust is almost reverential, like someone bearing a chalice.

A huddle of people bustles noisily into the wing. It's the doctor, trailed by a dozen students. The rubber soles of their white shoes screech against the floor. My bed is at the far end of the room. There are four or five patients between us, but he skips one and enters my cubicle. He's ridiculously young. He looks barely twenty. He goes straight to the card stuck to the wall, checks it against the chart on his clipboard and asks who I am, all without so much as a glance in my direction. He writes my name on the chart, looks at my bandaged hand and motions for the group to join him.

The closer the doctor's voice gets, the more nervous I feel, as if I were about to take an exam I hadn't studied for. They're going to assess whether I'm fit to keep living, to recover, to pick up a paintbrush again someday. The doctor's voice is firm, his accent staccato; he doesn't bother with niceties, though when he makes the occasional joke his disciples reward him with their laughter.

He stands at the foot of my bed and studies the report. I'm corralled by the students, who focus their attention on him, not me.

'Let's see. So what happened here, José?... Tried to get off the train before it reached the station, did you? Well well well! The cure was worse than the disease, am I right? Let's have a look at that hand.'

'No, doctor, I didn't want to kill myself or anything like that,' I protest as he unpeels the layers of gauze and exposes the swollen meat below. The stench snaps my head back like a sucker punch. I'm suddenly on the verge of tears.

'Is that right? How'd you get yourself so ground up, then? Says here you tried to commit suicide, according to the paramedics. That you threw yourself off some building and they found you dashed to pieces down below. Am I wrong?'

Fat tears squeeze from my eyes and a sob catches in my throat. I shake my head, which throbs like an enormous heart about to burst, not looking at him.

'Because if dying's what you wanted, it doesn't seem very smart to do it piecemeal. Just look at this – it's like a chorizo taco.'

He prods the skin with a pair of tweezers and my throat releases a booming cry that ricochets off the walls. I can't contain my tears any longer. I must look like a total wimp. What must these damn students think of me?

'You know, it looks to me as if you took a bit of a beating,' the doctor says. The others fall silent, waiting for me to say something. I stay silent.

The tears stop and I'm left only with a case of the hiccups.

'What did they hit you with? Do you remember? Do you remember who did it?'

My mind stays mute. It doesn't want to explain.

'Because if someone used you as a piñata, you'll have to file a police report, OK? You'll have to press charges if you want to be properly compensated, got it?'

No. My head asserts a solid, automatic *no*. I look down and decide not to speak at all.

'Fine. Well, we'll get to work on this hand and see if we can't save it,' he says, more to his students than to me. 'Two screws were inserted into the third and fourth metacarpals. The X-ray also shows fractures in the scaphoid and lunate bones, meaning a possible radio-carpal arthrodesis. If he responds to the antibiotic, we can continue with the orthopaedic procedures. Otherwise, well… we'll have to remove the whole extremity. Better to save a life than save the piece, don't you think?' He meets my gaze for a fleeting instant. 'The inflammation process is evident in all the muscles and ligaments. Necrosis is still limited to the skin. Let's hope it starts to diminish by tomorrow… Santos, put down that we need a clean wound and fresh dressing every two hours and a higher dose of Ciproflaxin.'

I devote myself to studying the name embroidered on the edge of his labcoat pocket, near his heart. The satiny curlicues of the double *m* in Emmanuel, the *h* in

Hernández. His words are so dire that I choose not to listen; I'd rather imagine a fountain pen tracing the florid calligraphy of letters that tell me nothing at all.

The doctor turns the page on his clipboard and proceeds to the next cubicle, flanked by his entourage, like a flock of tourists trooping through a museum. They forget me as soon as they reach the next scene, and I'm left alone with the stench of my own death. 'Just cut it off once and for all, get it away from me,' I think. But that's the despair talking. I need it, it's mine; I need to keep fighting. It must be saved. I'm shaking with fear. When I think that it belongs to me, is part of me, I picture it lying on the ground in the distance: a puppy hit by a car, a pigeon burst open. It remains motionless, utterly divorced from the anguish I feel. The pain is the only thing that brings it close and makes it real.

A university nurse comes in later for the first dressing change. It's so painful that I throw up the unsalted soup and lime jelly I've worked so hard to force down. After she washes my wounds with litres of iodine and gauze, the stench finally subsides, although I literally cry myself to sleep.

I wake up freezing. Night has fallen: I can see the dark sky through the little window. Lamps are lit in a few cubicles and silence reigns. Scattered voices whisper. I wonder what I have to do to get another blanket. Two more blankets, twenty blankets. I'm so cold that I can't imagine even a bed of coals would warm me. As I grope around the headboard for a buzzer or a bell so I can call the nurse, I see a very tall man walk by. He's wearing a blazer with leather elbow patches and a duckbill cap. It's him! The man I saw playing golf in the empty lot, the man with impish eyes.

He walks on. I hear his steps growing fainter as he crosses the wing and I stand up, determined to follow. My arm now hangs from a wheeled contraption that allows me to get out of bed. The wheels jam every few steps. I need to catch up with him. I need to know who he is, what he's doing here.

I reach the entrance to the wing. I can't see him anywhere. I peer down the broad corridor that circles the courtyard. The black and white tiles vanish into a distant vortex, but he's nowhere to be found; I can't hear his footsteps, either. I look into each of the other three wings emerging from the patio. In each of them I find the same panorama: silence, whispers, moans and white sheets. There's no one but the patients. I pause under the central dome. There's a scaffold at one end; I can make out someone suspended up above. I call out and ask him if he's seen a tall man passing through. Could it be the golfer himself…? No, it's not. There's a resemblance: the thick glasses, the way he carries himself. He's wearing a paint-spattered grey smock and holding a brush in his hand. He's been painting.

'Are you alright?' he asks, starting to climb down from the scaffold. 'Should I call Mother Juanita? She's the night nurse. If you need something she can help.'

'I'm fine, thanks. I was just wondering if you'd seen someone walk through here a couple of minutes ago. A man about your height, wearing a suit and cap.'

'No, definitely not. It would be strange if I had – visiting hours ended ages ago.'

'He looked about your age and was wearing glasses like yours.'

'I swear I haven't seen a soul since I started painting tonight. Why don't you let me walk you back to bed,' he offers, gripping the rungs and lowering himself down to the ground. 'You probably shouldn't be up and about so late. You need to rest so you can get well.'

'Did you paint those murals?'

'I did indeed. Gabriel Flores, at your service.'

'Your technique is extraordinary.'

'Why thank you,' he says, smiling, and we both look up to survey the dome. He lets out a tired sigh. 'I may have years of work ahead of me, but I think it'll be worth it in the end.'

'Of course it will! I'm sure of that.'

'Are you in the art world yourself?'

'I'm a painter too, but I make Renaissance copies... Well, I used to.' I nod to my hand, suspended in its contraption.

'That's awful! What happened?'

'You know the drill. An accident at work.'

'A tragedy! What does the doctor say? Will you be able to use it again?'

'They don't know yet. I have several broken bones, and... it does seem that there's still some risk of... of losing it.'

'Don't say that. Don't be pessimistic. Who's your doctor?'

'Emmanuel Hernández.' I immediately think of the calligraphy embroidered onto his pocket.

'Oh, don't worry, he's a fatalistic sort. He tries not to give his patients false hopes and sometimes he goes a bit too far. Rest assured, you're in the hands of a top ortho-paedic surgeon. I'm sure you'll recover. Just make sure you follow all his instructions, of course.'

I let out a sigh. This man has a better bedside manner than all the doctors I've ever known. I feel better just listening to him; less frantic, at any rate.

We sit on one of the benches in the courtyard. It's a clear night and crickets chirp among the rose bushes. The sharp silhouette of an occasional bat darts overhead.

'Renaissance, you say? I painted some Renaissance works in my student days. I suppose they weren't bad for a school exercise, but I never liked it. Sticking to a predictable, realist form – it made me feel boxed in. And I couldn't limit myself to the canvas. As you can see, my arm is used to more unruly strokes. My wife says she's relieved she married me, because if I don't make it as an artist, I can always pay the bills by painting houses.'

He laughs candidly. He's really quite old; it must be hard for him to climb up, climb down, carry paint tins and sweep those unruly strokes of his all over the walls.

'I can show you what I'm doing, if you like.'

He takes out a scale drawing of the work. It's a dome over four cantera stone arches. He's painted a night sky full of shooting stars. It looks like a scene from the Apocalypse.

'I'm painting a city ablaze on the edge of that arch. And on this side, about halfway, I'll paint a dismembered body falling from the skylight. A body splitting open from all the light inside it.'

'Interesting.'

'Why don't you come with me?'

I follow him up to the top of the scaffold. He opens a tin of yellow paint, stirs it with a mixer and wipes the damp bristles of a paintbrush on his smock. Then he hands me the brush.

'You help me paint the fire. Once it dries, I'll paint the ash-grey silhouette of the burning city on top of it. Meanwhile, I'll sketch the skeleton plummeting down from the sun.'

I take the brush and daub some yellow onto the wall. The colour is flat at first, like a coat on the wall of a house. Slowly, though, the yellow evolves into fire in my head, and I start to give it form. I feel loose and open in my gestures. The image takes over, and I stretch out

101

to spread the paint more freely, to become the blaze as it consumes the city, dense with shadows and shades of smoke. I feel pleasantly warm, as if I were walking among the flames. The heat makes me sweat and I start breathing hard as I put my whole body into it, my torso and arms and hands.

I watch Don Gabriel work on the skeleton. He traces the shape of a body onto the concave surface, a human form splintering in mid-air. The body is twice his size and so close to him that it feels almost supernatural the way the image – transformed by a few strategic brush strokes – finally acquires perspective.

Once finished, he sets the brushes to soak in a bucket and we make our way down the scaffold once more. He offers me a cigarette and lies down on the black and white tile floor. He studies our work. I stretch out beside him, hands crossed behind my head.

'Good fire,' he says.

'Thanks, but it's nothing compared to that skeleton you painted.'

'I'd say you have the gift of expressing the essence of things. *You're no mere copyist, you're a poet.*'

'Strange… that's exactly what he said.'

'He? Who's he?'

'Horacio, the antiques dealer.'

'The person you were working for?'

'Yes, he's the reason why I'm here. He's the one who hurt my hand.'

Reflexively, I glance at it – but it's gone. The bandaged stump ends at the wrist. I move my arm and feel my hand's absent weight. It's a clumsy stick waving in the air. I sit up, horrified, looking frantically every which way, as if someone had just made off with it.

'Easy, son, calm down,' Gabriel says, but I thrash around on the floor like a drowning man.

'They took it!' I shout. 'They cut off my hand!'

'Come on, now, let's not get carried away. It's not as bad as all that. You can still paint with the other one.'

I hold out my healthy left hand. I stare at it, opening and closing my fist. He's right! My left hand works just fine. Unbeknownst to me, all the abilities of my right hand have been transferred to my left. I'd be perfectly capable of painting anything with this hand. I feel relieved. My heart rate slows. I'm transfixed by the sight of my hand clenching and unclenching, drawing and writing with imaginary gestures.

'I don't mean to pry,' Gabriel says, 'but what happened exactly?'

I try to reconstruct it all as best I can, connecting the scattered pieces of past that have jumbled together in my head. I take a deep breath before I speak.

'It's all a bit of a blur, but let's see... I was working at Horacio's place. The antiques dealer. He'd hired me to copy *La Morisca*, a sixteenth-century painting attributed to Mabuse. Everything was going fine, though there were some ups and downs. I'd figured out a clever way to work around the problem with the panel. It was walled into a chapel, you see, made of stone and clay. The panel for the copy was outside – in the same house, but in the studio at the other end of the building. I'd had to copy much of the painting from memory, until it occurred to me that I could prime a bunch of stretchers I'd found lying around the place. Posters of the Virgin of Guadalupe, landscapes, sad clowns – I primed them all and painted the more complicated parts of the painting on top. I copied bits and pieces onto each stretcher, compared colour tests, practiced brush strokes, tested glazes and patinas...'

'Like an ant, piece by piece.'

'Exactly, yes, like one of those leaf-cutter ants. I'd memorise fragments of the painting so I could reassemble them on the panel, which was more or less from the same era, but older – which I had to erase, by the way, though it broke my heart… Anyway, I'm rambling. Like I said, everything was going well enough. I'd finished mixing the base colours and had started working on the details of the copy. To tell you the truth, it was a forgery. No more, no less. The antiques dealer, who was travelling at the time, wanted to pass off the copy as the original with the legitimate heirs of Mabuse's painting. Just imagine what that meant for me. I had to recreate not only the details and the wear-and-tear, the cracks, but also the whole spirit of the painting – the essence, you know, the identifying mark we leave on whatever we do without even realising it. And that was the part that wasn't working.'

'You were still yourself, instead of becoming *the other*.'

'Yes! Precisely. But I couldn't see it yet. I thought there was some flaw in my technique, or in the colours… And that's when I met her…'

'Who?'

'Isabel. His mother.'

6.

It was the first day of the rainy season. I knew her name because I had read it in a little notebook I'd found while rooting around in one of the boxes stacked up in the studio, full of albums, postcards and letters.

> My name is Isabel but it is spelled with a 'j'. After all, the 'j' and the 'i' are as alike as I am like Jezebel, the slut. I should expect that at any moment the prophet will come down and condemn me, that the eunuchs will throw my body out the window to be eaten by dogs, until only my skull and hands and feet are left to teach the heathens a lesson. But that's not going to happen. No prophet will come, nor will dogs feed on my flesh. All I can do is wait for death, like someone waiting for a bus at the station, or whiling away the afternoon on the doorstep until night falls and cools the air. I hope time will grant me that same relief.

As I was saying, I was worried because my sfumatos didn't look anything like they did in the original. I'd done endless tests with different paint brushes, with every solvent I had to hand, but there have must have been some other way of making the glazing look smoky. Then I remembered the goat's bladder trick Don Lorenzo had showed me during my apprenticeship with him in Tepotzotlán. You had to treat it in alcohol and then use the furry inside of the skin to blur the paint.

That was how Don Lorenzo painted the flesh tones on his gilded estofado carvings. He'd bend for hours over the little face of an angel or saint, his touch as gentle as a cloud, stroking their cheeks with the soft bladder-skin. Every now and again he'd bring it to his mouth to moisten it with saliva and when I remembered it was a goat's bladder I was at once amazed and disgusted.

When I went to the kitchen to ask Tona if she would do me the favour of bringing me a goat's bladder from the market, she didn't even deign to look up from the pot of creamed poblano chillies she was stirring with a ladle. I was beginning to gauge her moods, so I went to sit out on the terrace without another word. Within a couple of minutes she came over with coffee and a pastry.

'How do you expect me to get hold of a thing like that then?'

'I don't know, you could ask a butcher, couldn't you?'

'You think I've got time to go around talking to butchers?' she said in her mannish voice and customary tone – hostile but only semi-serious.

'Don't get cross, Tona. I only thought to ask you because it's clear you're an expert at choosing cuts of meat.'

'Well, I don't know about that. I'll see. But there's no way I'm cooking that filth, you hear? I'm here to cook for the owners of the house, not to see to the staff's every whim. If you're so desperate to eat offal, you're better off going somewhere they'll serve it to you.'

I laughed. 'No, I don't want to eat it, I need it for the painting.'

She frowned, shrinking back as though she'd seen a spider.

'You use it like... like a cloth!' I mimed wiping a window in the air. 'I honestly wouldn't trouble you with something like this if I didn't need it so much. I'd go myself, but you know I'm running out of time. You've seen how rushed I am...'

'Well, if that's the case, I'll see what I can find.' She flung her plaits over her shoulders and went back into the kitchen.

So you can imagine my surprise when I arrived for breakfast the next day only to find a goat, alive and bleating, tied to a chair by its leg.

'What on earth?!'

'I didn't know which bit you needed, so I thought I'd better bring you the whole animal.'

'But... it's alive.'

'That's your problem, darling. You asked me for a goat's bladder and there it is, inside somewhere, full of piss.'

I scratched the back of my neck, bewildered. Had she done it on purpose?

'Well, never mind I suppose. We'll have to make birria,' I said, and sat down at the table next to the goat, which was tugging on its rope.

'That's not a bad idea, you know! I have a recipe from my comadre – she's from Sayula and makes the best birria in the world. If you leave me the meat completely clean, maybe I'll work up the energy to make it.'

If what you wanted was to make birria, then why the hell didn't you just buy a dead goat, I wanted to ask her, but it was best to leave the matter at that.

El Gordo came down for his plate of fruit, as he did every morning, and I asked him to come back when he had fed his macaw. Finishing my breakfast, I asked Tona for a knife, a whetstone, a rope and a washbowl. I set about sharpening the knife as I waited for El Gordo.

When I said I wanted him to help me slaughter the goat, he behaved, as ever, as though he hadn't understood. He stood there looking sideways at the animal with his restless pupils. I explained again and again what he had to do, but got no reaction from him. After I put the knife handle in his hand and gave him the instruction for the umpteenth time, I realised he was trembling. The knife clattered to the ground and he ran off to hide.

The cook laughed, poking her head over the countertop. 'You really thought El Gordo was going to help with that? As if. Let him be, he's not made for that kind of thing.'

When I was a child, I learned to slaughter chickens on the ranch, but I'd never killed a bigger animal. I'd watched my uncles butcher a pig once. Four or five of them grabbed it together and stabbed it in the heart. The animal's cries were like pins sticking in my ears. You could hear them on the other side of town, they were so loud and desperate.

But the goat was only the size of an average dog, so I decided on the same method we'd always used with the hens. I tied its feet together and took it to the back of the garden, under the trees, where there was dry earth to absorb the blood. I hung the animal from its back feet so it was suspended about thirty centimetres off the ground, then dug a shallow hole underneath it. It didn't bleat. It seemed to be waiting for something. It wagged its tail like a happy puppy.

I crouched down by its head and grabbed the knife. I wanted it to suffer as little as possible, so without putting it off any further, I grabbed its ears with one hand and thrust the blade in under its jaw to slash open the throat. The blood spurted vigorously onto the earth. The spatter on my trousers and shoes blended in with the spots of paint. Without letting go of the animal's head, I looked up. Sun angling through branches. Then its death rattle began. Its front legs kicked up and down like a lever. When it was finally completely limp, I untied the rope and re-hung the goat, legs akimbo, at a better height to butcher and skin it.

The sight of the blood had quickened my pulse and stood my hair on end. I carefully slit open the stomach until I could see the innards. The heavy smell of the intestines made me lightheaded, like I'd been breathing in solvent. I let the innards tumble into the hollow in the ground, along with the blood, and set aside the heart, liver, and bladder in the washbowl.

I was on my way to the tap to wash my hands when I saw her.

She was walking through the garden in high heels. Eyes fixed on her feet, she gathered up the full skirt of a light cherry-coloured dress in her hands. Her hair was tied high on her head, her pale skin glowing in the sun like a ghost in an antique photograph. She stopped at the mouth of the cave, opened the gate and lit a candle. She pressed her hands to her chest and began praying quietly, murmuring things I couldn't hear, hidden as I was behind the trees. She looked like the kind of funereal sculpture you find in cemeteries. Occasionally she squeezed her eyelids as though to stop them stinging bitterly, although perhaps I imagined this – it would have been hard to see such a thing from a distance.

I didn't want to interrupt her prayer, so I went back to work without rinsing my hands. Although it was my first time skinning an animal, I didn't find it too difficult. The hard part was the heat, which had started in earnest. Within five minutes I was drenched in sweat and flies were biting my forehead and arms, swarming the pool of offal and blood. The smell grew more and more revolting.

From one moment to the next, great dark clouds thronged the horizon. I'd have to get a move on. It thundered, like boulders crashing together inside the clouds. The light turned grey-yellow, yellow-grey. I was unstringing the goat when the first drops struck the earth, but instead of running for shelter I just let the deluge wash away all the filth, all the blood, sweat and flies.

That sudden coolness left me euphoric. I felt like running, jumping in the puddles, gulping down the fat drops as they fell from the sky. But as I went out into the clearing I stopped short: she was still there, at the mouth of the cave, crumpled like handwriting half faded by the rain.

I left the tray of meat on the kitchen countertop, took an umbrella from the hatstand in the corridor and went to get her. I helped her to her feet, holding the umbrella over her head. But when she saw we were heading for the terrace her body went rigid and she refused to go any further. Her bones felt like they were made of something soft and pliant. 'Let's go inside, you'll catch a cold,' I said to her, but she dug her bare heels into the ground. 'I don't want to go back to the house,' she said. So we took shelter in the studio instead.

The storm intensified, the rain turning to hail. The transformers fizzed and we found ourselves suffused with the grey tint of the afternoon, the garden fashioning shadow plays for us. I didn't know what to say. I hardly dared open my mouth. I took the sheet off the bed, draped it round her shoulders, and took her to sit in the little living room. Then I went to the kitchen to find something hot for her to drink. As I stood in front of the stove waiting for the water to boil, I thought *She's like a little damp bird*, and felt a wave of pity and affection for her.

I put the mug in her hands and asked if she needed anything. She shook her head. She refused again when I asked if she wanted me to go and find Tona, if she wanted to change into some dry clothes, if she was hungry. I let her keep staring out vaguely at the rain for as long as she wanted, and went about my work. I needed to make the most of what little light was left to wash the bladder properly, rinse it under the tap, scrape off any adhesions with a knife. Finally, I plunged it into a Nescafé jar I'd filled with cheap tequila I'd found lying around in an unlabelled bottle.

The rain started to ease. Isabel stood up, wandered around the studio a couple of times and went over to the panel where I was making the copy.

'It's her, isn't it?'

'Who?'

'Her. Nut.'

'La Morisca'?

'Nut, Urda, La Morisca… whatever you want to call her.'

'Yes. I mean, it's a copy. Remember I told you?'

'You mean… But that's impossible! When you told me Horacio had hired you I imagined you were going to copy his Modigliani again, or something by Remedios Varo, or, I don't know, something else. I never thought it would be her.'

How odd. She talks about the painting as though it's a person, I thought.

'I imagined her very different,' she said, examining the woman's face.

'You mean you've never seen her before?'

'No.'

111

'Well supposedly this should be identical to the original. If it's not, I'm done for.'

'But why would my son want you to copy *this* painting? I don't understand. What for?'

'I'm afraid I don't know,' I lied. 'All I know is I haven't enough time to finish it before the deadline. But I'm surprised you don't know the original piece. I can show you, if you like.'

She hesitated for a few seconds.

'Could you really do that?'

'Of course, I have the keys to the chapel. Come, I'll show you. Although there's no way of lighting the place except with candles.'

'It's just that I don't... I don't want them to see me out there. I don't want them to know I'm here, with you.'

'Do you mean Señora Tona?'

She nodded.

'Don't worry, I think she's gone out. When I went to the kitchen just now she wasn't there. Do you want me to check?'

She nodded again, looking frightened. I finished clearing up and went over to the house. I called out to Tona several times with no response. She wasn't in. I returned to the studio for Doña Isabel. I took her arm and held the umbrella in my other hand. We went into the chapel, and I lit the altar candles and watched her contemplate the painting, suspicious, like a cat confronting its own reflection.

I too went over to look at the painting for the umpteenth time, only now without an eye to whatever detail I had to copy next. I saw the whole image from a different perspective, with the composure of a tour guide showing off a city he knows inside out. I could never have imagined this would be the last time I saw it.

'Do you think she's better than me?'

'Of course not, a work of art can never be worth more than a person.'

She shrugged and then burst into tears. There was nothing to do but to offer her a hug and absorb her shuddering sobs. The kind of violent crying you hear at a funeral, choked back in shame.

I waited until she'd calmed down and then said we ought to get back because Tona might arrive at any moment. I stuck my head out onto the terrace to check the coast was clear. The grey of the night was growing heavier overhead. We were about to venture into the garden when we heard the sound of the front door. Doña Isabel immediately pulled me towards the house. I barely had time to close the umbrella. I followed her down the corridor. Past the door of her room, then Horacio's door, there was another door out to a courtyard I'd never seen before. An empty courtyard, up against the back wall of the property. To the left was Isabel's French window and opposite was a single tree, a jacaranda with a twisted trunk, next to a collection of large clay pitchers piled against the wall.

In the corner of the courtyard there was a little alleyway, half a metre wide, that led to the garden. It allowed us to reach the studio without Tona seeing us.

The furtive journey around the property seemed to have given Isabel a new lease of life. Her cheeks were rosy and her eyes bright, still glassy with tears. She sat by the window with her knees pulled up on one of the Miguelito armchairs and sighed deeply. I imagined she was exhausted.

After a while she asked if she could use the bathroom. I went in ahead of her to give it a once-over, grateful that the growing dark would hide the mess. I flushed the toilet, took down a pair of trousers that were hanging on the towel rack, and told her she could go in.

I heard her turn on the shower. She was going to be a while. I checked the shelves for some way of illuminating the room and found an old pipe that I filled with oil and lit. I left it in the bedroom so she'd have enough light to get changed by. It was almost seven p.m. – I hadn't eaten since breakfast and the rain had awoken my appetite.

'Jesus, Mary and Joseph, what a storm!' exclaimed Tona when she saw me come into the kitchen. She was putting the goat in a bag so she could store it in the fridge. 'I only went to Atemajac to get some chillies but then the heavens opened. And it gets so bad over there… every street flooded, drains spouting water up to here.' She held out her hand about a metre from the floor. 'And halfway across the stream El Gordo's truck gives out. That man'll be the death of me. Completely useless. I had to come back in a taxi. I just hope the canal doesn't overflow, because if it does El Gordo'll be done for, truck and all.'

'Gosh, well I'm glad you're back, Tona. But what about El Gordo? Should I go and give him a hand?'

'No, don't be daft. Let him tie himself in knots. I do need you to help me get the power back on, though. Every time there's a blackout the fuses blow. It's only a matter of changing them, but the wires make me nervous. Come.'

We went into the laundry room and Tona pointed to a red metal box inside a cupboard.

'There are spare fuses and tools in there.'

I rooted around in the box while she started pulling the ribbons out of her wet pigtails.

'The switch is upstairs.'

I followed her up the spiral staircase. Although she kept the rest of the house in perfect order, Tona's own room was a real hovel, both dirty and untidy. The cement floor was cracked, the bed unmade, and there was a mountain of clothes heaped on a chair. On a dressing table with a mirror, a clapped-out old TV set competed for space with countless pendants, ribbons and other trinkets, jumbled among rancid creams and perfumes. On the wall, next to the cross above the headboard and the little altar bearing the Virgin of Zapopan and a baby Jesus, hung her matching heavy velvet skirts and tops, their bright embroidery and lace petticoats peeking out the bottom, each encased in a murky, dust-covered plastic bag. We went up to the roof and it was a relief to breathe the clean air in the aftermath of the rainstorm.

The fuse box was in a corner by the sink, under the shade of a little tiled roof. I flipped the switch and opened it gingerly. The glass tubes were completely fried, letting off an acrid blue smell.

'Once, when I was little, there was a blackout at my mum's house and I touched the naked cables trying to sort it out,' Tona said, shining a torch over my shoulder. 'And well, I could've burned myself to a crisp. Ever since then they've made me nervous.'

'Do you have other siblings or is it just you and El Gordo?' I asked her as I pulled out the first fuse with a pair of pliers.

'There were ten of us. We were the youngest, but, El Gordo being how he is, it was up to me to look after Mum. That's the custom there, in Juchitán – the youngest has to learn how to run a respectable household. Before I could even talk properly I already knew how to tie my underskirts, light the stove and wash the beans. After a while you learn to enjoy these things and even get a taste for dressing up. These days some muxes even get surgery.'

'And what brought you all the way up here?' I felt like chatting while I changed the fuses – I was only on the second.

115

'My mum died very young. She got cancer, and there was no way of saving her. I stayed by her side day and night. We buried her on my fifteenth birthday. They were going to throw me a quinceañera, but it never happened in the end. Since all my other brothers and sisters were married, there was no one else for me to look after, so El Gordo and I came here with an uncle who worked as a gardener. And we've been here ever since.'

'It's been a while then, hasn't it'?

'We turned fifty-five last month. Horacio, bless him, even brought me a mariachi band and a giant bouquet of flowers.'

'You'll be retiring soon.'

'I suppose, but I don't want to. It wouldn't make sense – I don't have anywhere else to go. Some of my siblings are dead, others went to the US. My oldest brother lives in Los Angeles and said I should join him there, we could open a Oaxacan restaurant. But only I could go. El Gordo would never make it over the border. And besides, the señora needs me here. I wouldn't leave her for anything in the world. I always say it was fate. Life robbed me of one mother only to give me another to care for. Because it doesn't matter that we're practically the same age, that she's only three years older than me – as far as I'm concerned she may as well be my real mother.'

'Is she sick, or…?'

'No, not at all. She's never been sick. The only time she was unwell was when Horacio was born. You've no idea the fright she gave us… she almost didn't make it. And on top of that, the baby was all feeble, he wouldn't eat. The poor thing was drier than a stream in April.'

'I only asked because she never leaves her room, does she?

'She's been like that since Don Socrates died. You should have seen her when she was young. So full of joy…'

'Really?'

'Don Socrates used to say she wrote lovely poems. And it's not like she had it easy, you know. You might think so because they're a rich family, but God knows she struggled when she was young. She was orphaned at twelve years old. Her parents were attacked by bandits on the highway. And her uncle, who became her guardian, was a good-for-nothing who spent her inheritance in the blink of an eye and was never heard from again. But despite everything, she was always a God-fearing woman. I thank the Lord for putting her in my path. I sometimes wonder what would have become of me if it hadn't been for her.'

'So you started working here as soon as you arrived in the city?' I finished screwing in the fuses and started changing the electrical tape on the dusty, cobwebbed cables.

'No, first I went to Don Socrates's house, but his mother didn't want me there. Because I'm a muxe, you see? She treated me very badly. She'd get cross about every little thing and said she was going to throw me out in the street. I was scared because she had witch in her – if I didn't iron a shirt properly she'd slap me and say the barn owl was going to come and peck out my eyes. But then Don Socrates met Isabel, one day when she was selling sweets in front of the church in Chapalita. He went up to her, asked her name and where he could find her again. She said she was with the Capuchin Poor Clares and he arrived the very next day to ask for her hand. They had such a pretty wedding... When they went to live together she asked her husband if I could go with them. We were still in the house in Santa Tere back then. When the baby was born they built this place and we came to live here. Oh, those were happy days. She'd go to parties or to the club, and then sometimes she'd come home and say to me, "Tona, on Sunday we're going to throw a cocktail party for two hundred people," and I'd run around like a headless chicken preparing canapes, tablecloths, drinks…'

'And then what happened to her?'

'Well, Señor Socrates died, you see…'

'But that was a long time ago, wasn't it?'

'Sometimes neither life nor death can bring peace. Perhaps she'd be able to move on if her husband had had a normal death, like anyone else, but the problem is he's still there.'

'What do you mean he's still there?'

'Well, you know, his soul, his spirit. You know what I mean. Here, let's flip the switch and see if that's done it.'

I flipped it, but nothing happened.

'It must be the transformer.'

'Hard to believe we live in a rich neighbourhood, isn't it? Leave the switch where it is, I'll push it up early tomorrow morning with the end of a broom, I don't want the fuses blowing again when the power comes back on.'

Back in her room, Tona took a brush and began combing out her long grey hair.

'There are candles downstairs in the pantry, take what you need. I'm going to turn in now, I feel like I'm coming down with a cold. Don't leave the fridge door open for too long, will you? Who knows when the power will kick in again, and I don't want that meat to spoil.'

I said goodnight and pulled the door shut. I went down the spiral staircase and felt around for candles on the top shelves of the pantry. I lit one in the kitchen so I could put together a plate of fruit, bread and a bit of cheese. I blew out the flame before leaving but then came back to tuck a bottle of something under my arm – it might have been rum, or Don Pedro brandy or maybe Licor 46. I couldn't see a thing.

Isabel had finished showering and was lying curled up on the edge of my bed, wearing a bathrobe I'd been using. It had probably belonged to her husband or her son. Her hair was wet, fanned out on the pillow. She was watching the gentle flicker of the altar candle. I told her I'd brought her something to eat, if she wanted it, but she didn't.

'She didn't see us?'

'No, I've just been talking to her. I had to go up and change the fuses. You've nothing to worry about.'

I let her be. I went to the living room and served myself a glass of whatever it was I'd brought under my arm, but I couldn't identify it from the taste either. It was probably expensive, something like sherry, but less sweet, more delicious. I put my feet up on the table, folded my arms over my chest and sat there listening to the dripping of the night.

I woke up stiff with cold before dawn, god knows what time. Without thinking, I went and got into the bed where I discovered her warm, slight body. She didn't move at first. Then, as I was drifting off, she rolled over and clung to me, soft and smooth like a caterpillar on a branch. Her face was so close to mine I could breathe in her exhalations and match them with my own quickening breaths, struggling to contain a roar that rose up from some vague organ at the centre of everything. I thought, 'She's got nothing on under that dressing gown,' and then I could no longer stop myself.

I kissed her lips and reached between her legs. Her flesh felt like it might come away in my hands. My blood was ablaze, knowing it was her, the unreal, the unreadable. It was like I was still dreaming, ready to surrender to the longing that had set me aflame. Little by little, after long months of neglect, my desire unravelled itself. She straddled me and I gave in to the swell of her body.

When I opened my eyes, she was already awake, and had been for who knows how long. She was staring at the ceiling.

'It's nice here,' she said. 'The silence isn't like the kind you hear in the house. It must be the smell of paint. It makes you feel like you're in a cabin in the middle of the forest.'

She wriggled her warm body down under the covers and curled up in the crook of my arm. Her aging body made me feel embarrassed, sour as a hangover, but instead of recoiling, I drew her in and brought my nose to her forehead. Her hairline smelled like marzipan or biscuits and reminded me of my childhood.

She got up first, to go to the bathroom, and I followed. When I went out into the studio I found her sitting in the living room eating a bunch of grapes.

'You did well to bring my husband's port,' she said, pointing at the bottle on the table and smiling. 'Somebody ought to enjoy it.'

She sat in an armchair with her legs tucked under her. Dressed in my sweatshirt and trousers, she looked like a little girl, much younger than she was – or perhaps that's just what I wanted to believe, to soften my regret.

'The power's back! Could you put some music on?'

'Sure, what would you like to listen to?'

'Anything. Something cheerful but not noisy.'

'Cheerful, but not noisy,' I repeated, 'let's see…'

'Anything, really.'

I put on one of the records I'd played most often, one by Louis Armstrong, and she approved.

I went to the kitchen for pastries and coffee. The lawn was soaking and I had to take my shoes off to cross it. The macaw's happy squawks could be heard from the back of the garden and Tona was singing along, quietly but melodramatically, to a José Alfredo song on the radio.

The smell of garlic and adobo was wafting from the kitchen, the broth on the hob diffusing the air as far as the terrace with a rich, salty hint of sweat or sex.

'Morning. How's your cold today?'

'Better, thanks. I put some potato slices on my temples last night and by morning they were burnt to a crisp. Will you be having breakfast? Because it's not ready yet. I've got to get this done first.'

'Don't worry. Maybe later. For now I'll only trouble you for some coffee.'

'Now, that we do have. Hang on, I'll get you some.'

She opened the oven to insert a large clay dish covered over with banana leaves. It looked too heavy for her, but as she bent down to hold it at knee height, the muscles in her arms taughtened for a moment, accentuating her masculine features.

I went back to the studio with a pot of coffee and the basket of pastries. Isabel took a concha and nibbled the sugar off the top in silence. I felt like a perfect idiot. I didn't know if I ought to say something about the night before or if it was better to keep quiet. I took a sip of coffee and then offered her the handle so she could drink too.

'It's been a long time since I listened to music. You've no idea how much I needed it.'

'You probably haven't been out dancing in a while then, either. I'll take you out, whenever you like, to Copa de Leche, Casino Veracruz – '

'Oh, you do make me laugh.'

'I mean it!'

'Careful, one of these days I might just take you up on that.'

'As soon as I finish the painting, you'll see, we'll make it happen.'

'Oh, I can't believe an artist like you is painting

121

copies. You're very talented, José. You should be making your own art.'

'If only. Unfortunately, not everyone is of the same opinion. It's hard to get people to buy my own pieces and well, what can I do, a man's got to eat.'

'Of course. But still, you don't know how I envy you. You're young, you can do what you like, go where you like… and I'm a fifty-eight-year-old woman with nothing to look forward to except being locked up in this house, which isn't even mine, it's *hers*,' she said, nodding at *La Morisca*.

'Well, I'll tell you one thing: you're very attractive for your age, if you really are fifty-eight. Besides, there's no need for you to be locked up, there are hundreds of things you could do. You could go travelling, set up a business, or get involved in a charity to help starving artists.'

We laughed.

'No, goodness, it would be a complete disaster. Just imagine – I was brought up by nuns. The only thing I know how to do is pray and make sweets.'

We laughed again and then fell silent for a few moments.

'No…' she said, drawing out the 'o' in desperation. 'The truth is I can't go outside. You've no idea how many people have a grudge against me out there. Some alive, some dead… I don't know which is worse. I'd have to go very far away, somewhere nobody knows me and where I know nobody. A place where people aren't like they are here. But there's no way. I just couldn't. I wouldn't even know how to get to the airport.'

'Well, you can count on me. It's no trouble at all. Just tell me what you need and – '

There was a bang from inside the house. A wooden bang, like a door or a piece of furniture. A clattering. We were suddenly alert. Isabel ran to hide in the bedroom, and a couple of seconds later I saw Tona stalking across the garden in a rage, not even bothering to lift her skirts up out of the mud.

'Where is she?!'

'What's happened? Who?'

'The señora! Doña Isabel! She's not in her room. I've looked all over the house and she's not there. She must be here, you've hidden her. Out of my way!'

'I haven't hidden anyone. What are you talking about? Calm down, Tona.'

She looked in every corner of the studio, then burst into the bedroom, crouched under the bed, slammed the bathroom door.

'Are you sure you haven't seen her? You didn't see her yesterday afternoon? Her shoes were lying in the garden. Lord help me, this cannot be happening.'

'No, Tona. I haven't seen anybody. I was cleaning the goat, then it started to rain and I came in here. I mean, I did see the shoes, but I assumed they were yours.'

'Mine?! You really are the stupidest man. Why on earth would I have fancy shoes like that. Oh, sweet Jesus have mercy… What am I going to do now? What if she escaped while I was out?'

'Calm down, Tona, if the señora is barefoot she can't have gone far. Maybe she just went out for a walk.'

'Lord, you are full of rubbish. Don't you get it? She can't leave! She hasn't left her room in over twenty years and you come out and suggest she's gone for a stroll… Mother of God, where could she be. Señor Horacio will die if he finds out. He cannot hear about this, you understand?'

'Don't worry, I won't say a word.'

'Oh, but what if Horacio arrives and we haven't found her? We'll have to call the police, the Red Cross.

How many times have I told him we need a proper phone, but he's so stubborn! I'll have to go to the police box to get an officer to come, search the area, bring those sniffer dogs they have…'

'Horacio won't be back for a while, Tona, why don't you do a proper search here in the house first. Check in all the nooks and crannies. She must be somewhere, I'm sure of it.' I led her to the door. 'Give me moment and I'll help, if you like, just let me get dressed and I'll catch up with you.'

'I'm going to fetch the police, that's what I'm going to do!'

'They won't listen to you, Tona. It's better I go. You look for her here, and while you do I'll go and talk to the police, ask if they've seen her. I'll have a look round the area too, what do you say?'

'And how are you going to recognise her, might I ask? You don't even know what she looks like!'

'Err… with a photo,' it occurred to me to say, to dodge the issue.

'Fine. You get dressed while I go and look for a photo.'

She went back to the house, and finally I could breathe.

Isabel was curled up in the bathtub with the curtain pulled halfway across.

'I have to go and pretend I'm talking to the police,' I told her. 'I'll be back in a couple of hours.'

I went over to kiss her forehead, to smell her hairline once again. She stopped me, touching my face. She looked at me closely and said would I please go to her room tonight: I could get in through the courtyard with all the clay pitchers, she'd leave the French window open and wait for me with bated breath.

7.

Outside, I didn't know what to do, where to go, or how to kill enough time that Tona would think I was looking for Doña Isabel – who would surely be back in her room by now, taking a bubble bath and lathering herself with creams.

I would have liked to run into Socket and listen to his crazy stories for a while. But that wouldn't happen until much later, until I'd returned from a long, strange adventure. I trudged aimlessly around the neighbourhood, which meant I risked running into the cops who'd harassed me. A little exercise would help clear my mind. The pavements, wet from the previous day's rainfall, were deserted, as they always are in neighbourhoods where people only travel by car.

I thought about going to find Felipe. I wondered whether he was still in town, what had become of him. I even thought about dropping by to see Mendoza at his studio, if only to shake hands and make peace. The time I'd spent cooped up in that house was reconciling me with the world – or had at least kept it so far away that certain things now felt less important. The tranquil house had softened me like sweet vinegar. You slowly dissolved into the silence and melted into something else, something that breathed inside, inhabited it.

Finding myself suddenly out on the street again, my perceptions expanded and made me feel vulnerable. The noise, the bustle, the lights. Everything felt like a threat, as if my bones were made of chalk. I was so distracted that I nearly got run over. I reached the avenue and considered which way to go next. If I continued downhill, I'd soon reach the cornfields of Zapopan. The slope was too steep on the other side.

I had some money in my pocket, so I indulged in a taxi downtown. I wanted to see people, drink coffee on a terrace somewhere, keep my mind busy. I got out by the university, at the corner of Munguía and Vallarta. I cut across the esplanade in front of the Templo del Expiatorio and sat under an umbrella at the café I used to frequent. It was nearly noon and quite hot. I ordered a large strawberry horchata. As soon as the brimming glass was placed before me, I heard the strumming of a guitar behind me. It was Malinche and her latest boyfriend. She leaned into the microphone: 'We'd like to brighten your day with a lovely ballad by Silvio Rodríguez, which goes like this...' I thought of making a break for it; at any other time I would have. I couldn't stand those corny, lilting tunes. But I was so comfortable that I would have endured that plus a horde of street acrobats.

Malinche gave private English lessons for a living – which is why she was named after Hernan Cortés's interpreter. Sometimes she'd get herself hired for a whole semester at the Instituto Torres Andrade. When she couldn't find work or didn't feel like working, she'd sing for money in cafés. But ever since she got together with that sandal-wearing hippie, she spent almost all her time busking on pavements or on buses, pretty much a charity case.

As their song came to an end, the couple approached the tables one by one. La Malinche came up to mine and greeted me with theatrical enthusiasm. She asked how I was, what was I up to, and I said I'd been working, same as always.

'Why don't you join me? My treat. It's awfully hot,' I said, and she accepted at once. She waved her boyfriend over and took a seat. He finished patrolling the tables she'd skipped.

'I'm so glad to see you, you have no idea. It must be fate. I wanted to tell you about an amazing idea I've had. I know you'll love it.'

Her boyfriend dragged over a heavy wicker chair from another table and tried in vain to find a patch of shade.

'You know Fredy, don't you?' We acknowledged each other tepidly. 'He paints, too. He's in his second year of Visual Arts.' Then she addressed her boyfriend. 'Believe it or not, José's already in the big leagues, aren't you?'

'Come on, Malinche, you know how it is. I still have to lick boots like everyone else.'

'It's true! You've no idea how good he is. Once he even painted me like Goya's Maja. Though he's more into realist figurative stuff, like from the Renaissance.'

'Ah, so you must know the maestro Rogelio Santiago,' said this Fredy guy, and I looked at him nonplussed. 'He teaches at the university. The famous researcher, expert in sixteenth-century art?'

I shook my head indifferently and took a sip of my horchata.

'Can I have the usual?' Malinche asked.

'Of course, whatever you like.'

Whenever we were out together, she always ordered a banana split with chocolate ice cream only. If she got three scoops of different flavours by mistake, she'd send

127

it back. 'As far as I'm concerned, there's only one decent flavour,' she'd declare. Fredy ordered lemonade and I tacked on a club sandwich, since I hadn't had breakfast.

'How's school going?' I asked, mostly just to rile Fredy.

'No, wait, this is what I wanted to tell you about! I stopped teaching because Fredy got this fantastic gig. He and his team from the Teocalli studio were picked to paint a mural right by the student cinema. There was a contest and they won. The film school will pay for the paint and their scholarship. I mean, OK, it's not a load of money, but some of them have to travel all the way from Ameca and they'll get a travel allowance and some cash for beers. And we'll have the entire wall in the parking lot to express ourselves! It's huge, everybody will see it. It's crazy, even Don Gabriel Covarrubias is supposed to come to the opening. The only thing is that it has to be finished by the end of the year, so we'll be hard at it for the next few months. Why don't you join us?'

I'm pretty sure that Fredy tried to pinch her leg under the table.

'Wow, Malinche, that sounds incredible, but I'm totally snowed under right now. This is the first time I've been out in maybe two months. Otherwise I'd love to help.'

'Oh please, you always have loads of work. Isn't it time you did something more, I don't know, artistic? More independent, no price tag attached.'

'Part of our group's manifesto', Fredy interrupted, 'is precisely to repudiate the subjection of art to the bourgeoisie. Art should be for the people.'

I wanted to cut and run, but I couldn't bring myself to be rude to Malinche, so I had to sit and swallow a twenty-minute socialist disquisition. By the time he finished, I was at the end of my tether and more convinced than ever that art is a fundamentally elitist enterprise.

Finally, Malinche signalled to him in a way they both understood and he excused himself to visit the restroom.

'I didn't want to ask in front of him, but I was wondering if you could lend me fifty pesos. I'll pay you back next week... it's a woman thing, please don't make me explain.'

'You don't have to explain a thing, Malinche. I don't have much on me right now, but here, take this.' I slipped her the only bill in my wallet. A hundred. 'Why don't you take this and pay the bill. It shouldn't be over thirty. I hope it's enough for what you need.'

'Yes, yes, more than enough. Thank you so much.'

She tucked the bill into her bra.

'Really nice to see you, Malinche. Take care of yourself. Say goodbye to Fredy for me, won't you?'

I gave her a kiss on the cheek and stepped out into the infinite glare of the esplanade, its shadows knife-trimmed like a painting by De Chirico. The neo-Gothic Templo del Expiatorio with its pretentious spires made me think of Fredy's diatribe and I smiled, more bitter than amused. I made the mistake of glancing back at the table. They were eating the leftovers on my plate.

I only had a few coins in my pocket, barely enough for the bus. And since the buses don't even pass through the wealthier neighbourhoods, I had to cross all of Providencia on foot, full of empty lots and houses up for sale. Plodding along, I mused about buying one of those houses for myself. A duplex or at least a flat. What Horacio was going to pay me would cover the down payment; I could take out a bank loan for the rest.

A fair-skinned, green-eyed young real estate agent almost convinced me to sign on the spot for a house in a development with twenty identical constructions, all lined up along a treeless avenue. Small but well-designed, with a garage and a tiled roof over the front door. The living-dining area was finished in vitrolite, with a full kitchen at the back and two well-lit rooms upstairs. I could use one as a studio, the other as my bedroom. The living room could be a gallery and library. In the four square metres of dirt that served as a backyard, I could plant rose bushes and a lemon tree. I promised the woman I'd be back.

Reaching the Glorieta de Pablo Neruda, a stone's throw from Horacio's house, I recognised a grey mass slumped in a flowerbed under the hot sun. It was Socket. The light was still green, but I hurried across the street, dodging cars. He looked dead. He was lying face-down on a bed of dry grass, his back twisted, arms at his sides. I nudged his knee with my toe. He didn't react. I tugged on his jacket sleeve, but his arm flopped lifelessly to the ground. I leaned over him and pushed his shaggy hair out of his face. His cheek twitched. I turned him over and dragged him into the shade of a tree. His body was slack, his face blank, his mouth like spent coal. I glanced around for a water pump and found an empty container in a bin, which I then rinsed out and filled with water. First I wet his mouth under the stream. Slowly, he began to respond, to swallow on his own. After a few sips, he started coming to. I kneeled beside him for a few minutes. He didn't seem to recognise me. Vacant-eyed, he took glug after glug from the Tropicana carton.

'Socket, are you all right? Should I take you to the Red Cross or something?'

'My tooth. It's hurting again. You should have left me to die, I was finally starting to forget about it.'

'As if. What were you thinking, lying out to roast in the sun like this? You're all dehydrated.'

'My tooth is killing me.'

'That's what you get for being so filthy. You'd better go to the dentistry school and get it pulled.'

'They pull teeth there?'

'Well, the students'll use you as a guinea pig, but it's better than nothing – '

'My tooth.'

'Let me stop by the house – I'll see if I can find you something for the pain. Wait here.'

'My tooth – ' He burst into tears like an abandoned child. As if it weren't really his tooth that ached, but something else, some deeper grief.

On the corner of Paseo de los Parques, an airport taxi stopped to let me cross. I suspected nothing until I reached the house and sensed a different hubbub, whiffs of Horacio's perfume... he was home over a month early.

His luggage sat in the hall, beside his bedroom door. Tona came to carry them in. She shot me a furious glance as she passed, either because I was late or because she'd discovered I never called the police; who knows which. She stalked into the kitchen without a word, and I wasn't about to go looking for trouble, so I kept quiet too.

I paused at the door. Horacio was pacing around, opening and closing drawers.

'Ah, there you are! Well, you certainly look like you've recovered.'

I patted the paunch I'd developed since he'd been gone.

'As you can see, I came back a couple of weeks early to start preparing the piece for shipment. Everything's gone swimmingly. I have so much to tell you. Look at this – '

He showed me a grey device, heavy as a gun.

'It's a mobile phone. Everyone has one in Japan. You can use it to make calls from anywhere in the world.'

I opened the lid and a little green screen lit up. I pressed a few buttons, extended the antenna.

'Give me that, it's not a toy. This is what will finally make a civilised species of us.'

'So the deal went well…'

'Of course it went well! Now the rest is up to you. I can't wait to see the copy, but I'm famished. That stuff they give you on aeroplanes is disgusting. Everything tastes the same. Why don't you join me for a bite and I'll fill you in. Tona made birria. It's odd, she always makes birria before I come home from a long trip. And I didn't even tell her I was on my way! That woman will never cease to surprise me. Come.'

He pinched my cheek as he stepped into the hall and I followed him to the dining room. I had to figure out a way to bring up the cheque. I couldn't bear to mention the payment to Doña Gertrudis, my ex-landlady. To be honest, it was embarrassing. But the advance was important. I needed that money to get my pickup back from the pound.

We sat at the table and Tona placed a heaped bowl of birria in front of us both. We began eating as soon as she brought in a stack of hot tortillas wrapped in a cloth napkin.

'Let's have two Estrellitas, Tona. Birria should always be served with an Estrellita or it doesn't taste right.'

The beer was so cold that flakes of ice were floating inside the bottle.

'So listen. Long story short, the plan has been a resounding success. The heirs are thrilled and have already got everything arranged with customs. My Chinese partner is a delight, he's dying to meet you. If you want to go, he says he'll cover all your expenses and treat you like royalty – you can have a proper holiday. Then you can talk business if you like.'

'Oh great, thanks so much! I'd love to, obviously. I've always wanted to know what's on the other side of the world, see if everyone's really upside-down.'

'Not literally, but believe me, it's true – everyone really is upside-down. This is delicious, don't you think?'

I agreed. Mere hours ago, the piece of meat in the hollow of my spoon had belonged to a cute little animal that stood tethered to the table leg, bleating contentedly. But that didn't curb my appetite. On the contrary: the rich tang of the meat coated my tongue and the roof of my mouth, and my senses relished the subtle flavours of onion and chillies. Horacio was right: there was nothing better than the clean cool of an Estrellita to recover from the heat.

'So tell me, how's it going with *La Morisca*? If you didn't make a run for it after a couple of days, you must have everything under control. You're probably almost done, aren't you?'

'Come on, Horacio, did you really think I'd drop you in it? If I was going to do that, I would've said no right off the bat.'

'You see? That's why I like you. They don't make 'em like you any more, José. At least not in the world I live in.'

'Well, I'll be frank, Horacio, there's still a long road ahead. Details, finishes, the deterioration, the finicky stuff.'

'Forget about the deterioration. I couldn't care less about the details. What I care about is that it's really *her*. With what I'm paying you, I expect you to have brought Mabuse himself back to life.'

'Oh, by the way, that's another thing I wanted to talk to you about. There was an accident with the cheque you left me. It got... well, it was destroyed before I could cash it at the bank.'

'What do you mean, destroyed?'

'Yes, well, Tona accidentally put it through the washing machine – it was in my shirt pocket.'

'Tona! Tona, get over here!'

'It wasn't her fault, Horacio. It just meant I couldn't cash it.'

'Tona! What's this about you putting José's cheque through the wash? How many times have I told you to check the clothes before you put them in? How many times?'

Tona bowed her head, clutching her apron in her hands.

'You've no idea how many times she's done it to me, too. Are you stupid? Is there no way to get through to you, you imbecile?'

'Horacio, it's not – '

'Forgive me, Don Horacio, I promise it won't happen again.'

'You're senile. You don't even know what you're doing any more. I'm going to send you straight back to your village, mark my words. Just get out of my sight.'

He snapped his fingers three times and the woman retreated to the kitchen in humiliation.

'You're really something, my friend. So you've been working all this time with no advance payment? You don't scare easy, do you? God, I'm grateful to you, José, you have no idea how much this means to me.'

He barraged me with empty praise and plans as we lingered over the coffee and dessert we served ourselves; Tona had shut herself away in her room. Then we went to the living room in the studio and he rolled a couple of cigarettes with fragrant tobacco which we smoked in near silence, watching the light change on the other side of the window.

'What is this?' Horacio spat through gritted teeth. 'Please tell me this is some kind of joke.' He was standing in front of the copy of the painting. He'd flushed red as an alarm, a vein pulsing in his temple.

'It's not finished, Horacio. You can't judge it yet. It needs another month of work, just as we agreed at the start.'

'Time has nothing to do with it. This isn't what I asked you for, José.'

'You asked me for a forgery, an exact copy of *La Morisca*, and that's what I'm doing.'

'Right, yes. But this says nothing to me. This painting is dead!' he shouted.

'Horacio, please, relax. The volume and other effects will come through with the glazing.'

'Fuck your glazing. Where's the error, the accident? This painting may be identical to *La Morisca* but it isn't *La Morisca*. It has nothing to do with her, you understand? It's too… flat, too precise. You corrected Mabuse's hand instead of replicating it. It's like you've painted a wax statue, not a flesh-and-blood woman. Don't you see? That's exactly what the heirs are going to notice, not the cracks and stupid technicalities you've frittered away your time on. I bet you've been idling about all this time, living large at my expense. Don't think I'm going to pay you a single cent for this rubbish, you hear me?'

My stomach churned with rage. I couldn't take it any more.

'You know what, Horacio? I've already wasted too much time on this to put up with you behaving like a spoiled brat. Keep your copy and your money. I'm done here.'

'Oh, so now you want to leave me hanging! And you're threatening me.'

'No, I'm not threatening you. I just don't get your whims, I don't get what it is you want, and I won't tolerate you dismissing my work this way. I've worked hard, especially considering the conditions I was forced to accept. Or do you think it was easy to copy a painting that's locked up in a room twenty metres away? I've had enough, I don't like being exploited. I'm done here.'

'So you think you can walk away, huh. Just like that.'

'Look, Horacio, I'm sorry we haven't reached an understanding. Life's about to get a lot harder for me, I don't have anything at all out there. But I'd rather put an end to this. For dignity's sake.'

I turned around and started to collect my things.

'Dignity. Ha!' I heard him hoot from a distance. He had shut the door behind him before I'd even turned around. I heard the jangling of keys and the bolt sliding into place from outside.

I didn't understand what was happening. I rushed to the door and tried to open it, to no avail: I didn't have the key to the deadlock in my set. My forehead muscles trembled, tired from constant strain. The picture window comprised four large panes held together by a metal crosspiece. The pane that held the door was a sliding piece. That's how they'd managed to get the enormous panel for the copy inside. I tried to pull the sliding pane to the left and open the door, but it was no use. It had been secured with a padlock in addition to the steel bolts, and the metal rattled as I tugged. I gave the glass a few kicks, but all that did was hurt my foot. The pane was thick and wouldn't be easy to break.

I tried to calm myself down. That idiot! How could Horacio write off my work when I still hadn't finished? Too *precise*? What was that supposed to mean? I reckoned it had to be just one of his tantrums; nothing that couldn't be sorted out. If he wanted to keep me there, it must mean he didn't have anyone else to finish the forgery, so we'd have to negotiate. I picked up the bottle of port and took a swig. Then I filled a glass and nursed it, taking more measured sips, watching the afternoon fade into dusk. I considered the possibility that it was this ubiquitous violent light that made us act this way. Inflaming everything, refusing us rest.

I don't remember how late I fell asleep. I was a little drunk by then. When I woke the next morning, I checked the door right away; it was still locked, so I went back to bed. When I couldn't possibly sleep any more, I got up for some water from the tap and peered into the living room. Horacio was sitting outside, at the edge of the path, with his back against the glass and his elbows propped up on his knees. I stood beside him on the other side of the window. I could see the threads of his dressing gown flattened against the pane.

'I've been giving this a lot of thought,' he said, his voice muffled by the glass barrier. 'I need you to be completely honest with me, José. Are you up to the task?'

'I can try. That's what I've been doing all these months. I don't think my work is as bad as you say. You should at least wait until it's done before you judge, don't you think?'

He got to his feet and turned around to look me directly in the eye.

'No, José, you don't understand. The figure is hesitant. It isn't well drawn. The painting only emphasises that hesitation. The point isn't to copy a form, but to represent it, to anticipate its movement, the spirit within.' He gestured to the panel as if he were talking about a real person. '*Grasp the spirit, the soul, the appearance of things and beings. Effects! What are effects but accidents of life, not life itself?*'

He spoke as if reciting a lecture he'd learned by heart, a speech chiselled into his memory.

'Cause and effect.' He gestured as if weighing them in each hand. 'Don't you get it? They're indivisible. Without it, reality is false, like your copy. You paint without seeing, without perceiving the life of what you paint. *You do not penetrate far enough into the innermost secrets of form...*'

'I don't know, Horacio, I'm not following you. Maybe you should hire someone who knows more about this theoretical stuff.'

'Theoretical stuff?! You ungrateful fool, that's why I hired you — because you haven't been corrupted by all that stupid theory. I need you to understand! I need you to express her!' He jabbed his index finger against the glass, printing it with round little smudges.

'Forget it, Horacio. Just hire someone else and leave me out of it.'

'Look, we're out of time. You're going to finish that painting and it's going to be perfect. Otherwise you won't make it out of here alive.'

'What?!' I thought I'd misheard him.

'That's the deal now, José. You finish the painting exactly as I want it, or you don't make it out of this house.'

I didn't believe a word. It sounded like yet another of his tricks, a ludicrous threat. I'd had it with his histrionics. I think I even laughed in his face. How little I knew about what was coming.

'And if I finish, then what?' I demanded, defiant.

'You leave and that's the end of it.'

'No. I leave and you pay me what you owe.'

He gritted his teeth and thought for a moment. 'All right. I let you go and I pay you what I owe.'

'Deal.'

'Now stop wasting time.'

'Okay, fine. So open the door.'

'No. You're staying right here.'

'Are you insane? I have to go to the chapel! How am I supposed to forge the painting if I can't even see the original?'

'That's for you to figure out.'

He turned on his heel and walked away. I yelled all manner of insults, hammered at the glass, knocked over the furniture. I was even on the verge of destroying the painting – spraying it with solvent, setting it on fire – but in the end I held back.

I spent the rest of the day trying to find a way out. Breaking the glass wasn't an option. Horacio could be armed, could use his new cell phone to call the police at the drop of a hat. I'd have to sneak out quietly. First, I tried to pick the lock with wires, with hair clips, with another similar key, anything I could find. The bathroom window was too small for a person to fit through. The bedroom window was promising, but I'd have to scrape off all the plaster and remove the rusty screws.

Near nightfall, I found myself all but defeated by hunger and exhaustion. Then a new shadow appeared in the garden. A shadow I already knew and was horrified to discover here, standing before this other door.

8.

It was almost as dark inside as out, where the evening was still taking its last gasps of light. Panchito, Doña Gertrudis's nephew, approached the window, put his hands on the glass and peered in. I felt like a reptile trapped inside a tank in a zoo. A malicious smile crept across his face when he found me rooted to the spot in fear.

'Hello hello, how are we today? Fancy seeing you here.'

'What do you want?' I asked, defensive.

'Me? I don't want anything. I'm just doing my job.'

His voice was muffled by the glass, so I shouted 'What are you talking about? Why are you here?'

'I told you, I'm just doing my job, same as you. While you paint your little cartoons, I make sure you don't scurry off like the slippery rat you are.'

'Listen, scumbag, you got a problem with me?' I barked, squaring up to him through the glass.

'Woah, take it easy, mate. None of this is my fault, Señor Romero hired me as security. I should be thanking you, really, for landing me such a good job. That Romero's a real gent, isn't he? Just look at this house! So don't take it personally. What happened the other day – it's all in the past now. That said, I'd happily smash your face in again, so best you don't go asking for it, eh?'

'What about Horacio? Where's Horacio?' My voice rose and grew more desperate. 'Horacio! Come and show your face, you bastard!' I shouted, hoping he'd hear me all the way from his bedroom.

'Tsk tsk tsk… Take it easy, man, don't put me to work already. Horacio isn't even here, you know. He went to Puerto Vallarta for a few days. Said dealing with you was too stressful, and as you can see, he's left me in charge.'

By this time I was really freaked out. My mind raced, trying to unravel this tangled trap.

'How long have you worked for him? When did you meet him?'

'Let me think – since he came to your house looking for you one time. He told us all about you, how you're a crook and a freeloader, how you owed him a tonne of money and wouldn't pay up. He even told us he'd asked the police and found out you had a criminal record.'

I collapsed into a chair. 'And Doña Gertrudis believed him…'

'Well of course we believed him. Señor Romero is a respectable man. When he gets back, he's hiring me to be his permanent bodyguard. He's getting me a gun and Ray-Ban sunglasses.'

I could hear myself wheezing, like I'd just summitted some snowy peak. Seeing my grey reflection in the glass, I knew I was lost. I opened and closed my mouth, eyes bulging. A terrified, confused fish, suffocating to death.

I don't know exactly when it occurred to me to do it. I went over to my worktable and turned on the light. I poured a bit of rabbit-skin glue and a spoonful of titanium white into a can, then filled it with water, gave it a good stir, and hastily painted the inside of the glass with a broad brush. Panchito swore and threatened me on the other side, peering in through the gaps where the paint hadn't yet reached, as I smeared thick brushstrokes over his face.

I have only a few memories from the time I was locked up, and they're all pretty hazy.

I remember, for example, that I couldn't sleep the first night. My mind invented one conspiracy after another, each more terrifying than the last. Plus, I was hungry. Once I'd finally managed to doze off around five or six in the morning, I woke again to the soft weight of a pillow over my face. Panchito's knee was crushing my chest, his arms pressing down just hard enough. I heard the wild axe-blows of my heart trying to keep me alive, fading only with the sound of retreating footsteps.

I spent the next day curled up in a corner of the room, practically under the bed, clutching defensively at a pair of poultry shears. Nothing happened. Panchito didn't come back, but by now I expected him to show up at any moment and rob me of what little breath I had left.

I also remember the morning of the second or third day, by which point I was faint with hunger, stiff from crouching in my corner, delirious and desperate. When I heard someone trying to open the shutters of the bathroom window, I leapt up in fright and hid behind the door frame. El Gordo was trying to open the air vent with his clumsy hands so he could throw down a couple of oranges, which I ran to pick up. I dropped them and they rolled around on the floor. I stood on the edge of the bathtub to peer out, but he had already gone.

I bolted down the first orange practically whole. I bit into the peel and sucked out all the sweet juice.

143

Then I opened it up, tugging out the fibrous strands with my teeth, finally feeling some weight in my shrunken stomach. The second one I peeled properly and ate slice by slice, as slowly as I could bear. Finally, I sucked each of my sticky fingers and licked my lips, tingly and stinging from the juice.

I also remember the birds and grasshoppers went completely silent after Panchito arrived. There was only an insomniac rat chewing its way through the boxes of family mementos.

What I cannot remember, no matter how hard I try, is how on earth I managed to paint *La Morisca*, blind. The very thought of it seems absurd. Perhaps it never happened, or at least not in the way I can dimly reconstruct it.

It was the morning El Gordo threw me the oranges. I couldn't get back to sleep so I went out into the studio and turned on the lights. As I stood there looking at the painting, I realised it was true: she looked stiff and life-less. I don't know if it was the hunger or the delirium of my confinement that made me suddenly see that I had to reconstruct the shapes I'd memorised before the whole could really come together. I'd need to mentally reassemble the painting from an imagined reality. The trees and mossy ruins, the setting sun, the bright-cheeked woman whose face shone with hard-won, long-awaited exultation. That energy – an opaque sphere, a brilliant orb on the verge of erupting into light – contained the force of the universe itself. Her spirit spoke through her uneven eyes, the poignant strain in her neck. She held her breath, lungs full of wonder, breasts swelling against the shiny blue taffeta of her dress. The ends of her hair floated outward, gently electrified by the power of the sphere she held in her strangely calm hands. Hands that knew what they were holding and didn't show the slightest hint of fear or doubt.

I went over to the table then and there, turned on the lamp and started preparing paints, solvents, clean cloths. Horacio's stupid threat, Panchito's arrival, the money, my hunger, all of it melted away before the need to capture in paint what would otherwise end up bursting inside me.

What I didn't know was that Panchito had also been tasked with monitoring whether I was working or not. As I painted, I saw him scale the trunk of a nearby tree to peer in the top of the French window, where the white-wash hadn't reached. That morning, with the sun already high in the sky, I finally received a plate of food. Rice, beans and beef in salsa verde.

'As Jesus said, here, if a man will not work, he shall not eat,' Panchito jeered when he opened the door to let El Gordo in with the tray of food.

Great, the bastard's found God, I thought. I decided to ignore him and tuck in, trying not to overdo it and give myself indigestion. I kept the leftover tortillas, in case they decided to starve me to death again. I asked El Gordo if he'd bring me a pot of coffee and some aspirin. I had a dreadful headache. He complied, ignoring the sadistic guard who called me a poor little pampered girlie and asked if I wanted a lemon ice lolly too.

The coffee and pills finally cleared my head, and I went back to painting. Each brushstroke gave me a clearer sense of what needed to be done. As clear as if I myself were the original artist, as if I'd left my own self behind and become him – become his idea.

I may have spent fifteen days, twenty days or even more in that strange state of hypnosis, completely engrossed in the painting. I paused only to bring food to my lips and snatch a couple of hours' sleep before continuing. I didn't give a toss whether or not Horacio would like it or what he was up to. I don't think he even crossed my mind that whole time.

Luckily the stretchers were still in the studio, propped in a corner facing the wall. Horacio hadn't even seen them. I flipped them around and arranged them wherever I could find space, turning back every now and again to check some detail or spark some memory that evoked the other reality, the one I was starting to glimpse beyond the forms painted on the panel.

It was the logic of the drapery, the weight of the fabric, a blade of grass, the way the sunlight fell on the foliage, the number of petals on the little white flowers at the woman's feet – that sort of thing. The rest didn't matter. My hand had a life of its own.

After all those days of work, I could finally say that the painting existed. *La Morisca* existed, replicated, brought back into being. Although, to tell the truth, it was a different painting altogether. The original was far away, further than ever, imprisoned in the chapel. I don't know if the *Morisca* I'd just painted was so similar as to look different, or so different as to end up being the same. I still don't know. I'd never have the chance to compare them.

I woke to the metallic bang of the door and jumped out of bed with my heart in my mouth. The door banged again, more slowly this time. It shifted the air. The first rays of sun were peeping over the horizon and flocks of birds were abandoning the treetops. A cool gust of wind from the garden caught me off guard. It had been so many days since I'd breathed that air. All was calm – no sign of Panchito.

I patted my pocket to check for the keys with the snake amulet and crept towards the exit. I hadn't taken more than three steps on the wet lawn when I was stopped in my tracks by a sense of heaviness, a weight in my chest. I turned on my heel, went around the back of the house and snuck down the narrow alleyway. There was something secretive about the empty courtyard, something restrained, tucked carefully away, like a heart. *In the silence the pitchers were overflowing, swilling water over the wet ground.* The glass door was half open. The sheer curtains billowed gently in the wind, then dragged their wet skirts back over the earth.

I found Isabel crouched in a corner by the dressing table, gazing blankly into space. Her lips shifted as she murmured incomprehensible words, her body rocking back and forth. I said her name several times, but she seemed not to notice I was there. I took her face in my hands to make her look at me, but her eyes shifted away to the side.

'Doña Isabel, it's José, the painter, don't you remember me?'

She didn't respond. I felt a wave of regret, like I'd made a terrible mistake, caused irreparable damage.

'Look at me, it's José, remember? You were with me the other day, in the studio. You said the smell of paint reminded you of being in a cabin in the forest.'

Then she started to cry. Her eyes turned red, her face crumpled, and she sobbed openly. Her cries were thunderous. A mountain collapsing would have left me less shaken.

'You... you forgot about me too,' she was saying between hiccups. 'You abandoned me for her, too.'

'Forgive me, Isabel. I wanted to come but... Horacio, your son, he's out of his mind. He's had me locked up in the studio all this time so I would finish the painting. He even got someone to guard the door. I only just managed to escape.'

I wanted to hug her, but she pulled away, covering her face with her hands. As she shifted, I caught a stench of urine and damp, and I recoiled involuntarily.

'But look at you…' I went over to help her up, trying to ignore the stink. 'You need help, you need looking after.'

She was in a truly pitiful state. She seemed to have aged a century in just a few days. Her ashen skin was carved with deep wrinkles. Her mouth was a dry hole, almost lipless, her hair dry and faded.

'I'll be fine, don't worry. It's just one of my crises.'

'I'm so sorry things have turned out like this. I hope you get better soon. I… I didn't want to leave without saying goodbye.'

'Wait, don't go yet. Do you want to know what happened that afternoon of the rainstorm?'

'OK, but first, come, let's get you into bed.'

I wanted to make sure she could walk. I held out my arms and helped her to her feet. She hobbled for a couple of steps and then managed to straighten up, which was a relief. I took her silk dressing gown off the hook and put it round her shoulders. She threaded her arms into the sleeves and tied the belt before lying down gingerly on top of the covers. I folded the bottom of the quilt over her legs, and then sat down on the edge of the bed.

'That day was twenty-five years since my husband's death. Never in all those years did I think to go and ask his forgiveness. I always trusted in God's mercy, that he would forgive what I did to the poor man. And the thing is… OK, I'll tell you. But please don't repeat this to anyone, will you? Nobody can ever know.' She brought her fingers to her mouth and whispered her secret through them. 'I locked the gate. I left him for dead in there, just like he was dead to me. I was so jealous of that other woman. He abandoned me for her. He gave his life for her. First he travelled and studied, then he started meditating and finally he locked himself up, coming out less and less, looking weaker and weaker. I felt so alone.'

She stared blankly as she spoke, her eyes wide, as though she were recounting a dream she'd just had.

'How was I supposed to know what was going on inside of him, why he was abandoning me and his son for all that heathen stuff? Days would go by and I'd have no idea what he was doing down there. I used to imagine him travelling miles underground to talk to the Devil, down in the depths of hell. And then whenever he re-appeared, how was I supposed to know if that skinny, crumbling body was alive or not, if it still had his living soul in it? One day I couldn't take it any more and said to myself: "Let him stay there for good. If he doesn't want to be with me and look after his child, then he can stay there with her, since he thinks about nothing but her anyway." And I locked the gate.'

Perhaps she was delirious. Perhaps she'd invented the story so she'd have something to blame herself for, something to pray for all day long. I couldn't involve myself in it any more; it wasn't my place. So I shushed her and stroked her forehead, hoping she'd calm down enough for me to leave.

'Hang on, though, I haven't even got to the good part yet,' she said, her mood suddenly brightening, as though she was about to tell the punchline to a joke. 'I know you won't believe me — by this point you probably think I've lost my mind — but I'm going to tell you anyway. At least to hear myself say the words. That day of the storm — '

Suddenly I heard the door opening on the other side. Somebody was in the living area with the eagle claw-foot table and was about to enter the bedroom. Instinctively, I threw myself to the floor and slid under the bed. The door closest to me flung open and somebody strode from one side of the bedroom to the other. My heart pounded. I did everything I could not to breathe and prayed he wouldn't crouch down to look.

'Darling…'

'Shut up. Get out of the way,' I heard Horacio snap, before he checked all four corners of the room and left the way he'd come. I crawled out from under the bed, wanting to get out of there as quickly as possible, but Isabel held me back.

'Come here, don't go yet, I haven't finished telling you,' she said, raising her voice.

I feared she'd give me away, so I relented and sat down again on the edge of the mattress, trembling, my heart thundering.

'You won't believe me, but that day when I stood by his grave and asked him to forgive me, I heard his voice so clearly, as clear as you're hearing me now. It wasn't a ghost's voice – trust me, I know only too well what a ghost sounds like. No, it was Socrates's voice echoing around the stone walls. He said he forgave me. Well, he didn't quite say that. He said: "Come now, Isabel, calm down and stop being so ridiculous." Imagine what a fright it gave me – that's precisely the sort of thing he used to say! First I wanted to make sure it was him, so I asked if it was a demon talking with his voice, or if it was some kind of trick, because I could hear him too clearly for it to be a spirit. But no, it was him, I'm sure of it.'

Lying on her side, hands tucked into her chest, she spoke more to the window than to me. The light of her eyes was yellowish, dead.

'I thought, *His spirit is still so strong, he must be very angry, he's come for me.* "What do you want?", I asked, and he said he didn't want anything, that it pained him to see me, that he didn't want me to feel remorse for what I had done to him. He said, "Get on with your life, Isabel, forget what happened, it doesn't matter any more. If you knew what was on the other side, you wouldn't waste your time on prayers." I asked if his soul was at peace, if he was suffering.' Isabel took my arm and fixed me with a wan smile. 'He said he was at peace, except for a terrible toothache. Of course he did – toothache is how unbelievers get punished in Purgatory. I've always known that, Mother Socorrito taught us. And there's no way my Socrates was going to heaven, heretic that he was. So there he is, suffering all kinds of torments, poor man. I told him I'd bring a priest to bless his tomb, that I'd hold a mass for him, and he replied he didn't want any of that. I said, "At least let me pray for the salvation of your soul," and he replied, "Oh stop being so self-righteous, woman. Your prayers do nothing but annoy me down here. Get on with your life as best you can. Enjoy what's left of it, there's no need to pray any more." I swear to God, that's what he said.'

'Well, that seems to me to be good news, don't you think? Now you can feel free to do whatever you want.'

'I tried, but then you abandoned me.'

'No, I told you, it wasn't my fault. Your son locked me up, he's lost it, I swear. I think he wants to kill me.'

'It's her. It's always about her. She's what matters, not me. She's always taking what little I have and leaving me with nothing.'

'Come on, that's not true. You have to understand, it's just a painting. If you didn't matter to me, I'd already have left. I wouldn't have come looking for you, would I?'

'Take me with you, José. Get me out of here. Please, I beg you. I can't stand being locked up a moment longer. What will I do now? Without prayer, without living out my penance, what else can I do? Please, take me with you!'

She sat up, her voice rising sharply. I was afraid we'd be discovered, that Horacio would come back and find me there. I had to get out however I could.

'Calm down, Isabel. I promise I'll come for you as soon as I can.'

'But what am I supposed to do until then? How will I bear the silence, now, on top of everything…'

It was like watching someone lost in a crowded station.

'You have to get better, and I promise I'll come and see you, alright?'

She lowered her head for a few moments.

'Can you fill up that glass of water and pass me my medicine?'

I filled the glass at the bathroom tap and took the dropper bottle, the one I'd brought her the first time we spoke, out of a little drawer she pointed me to.

'How many drops?'

'Just leave it, I'll take it in a minute.'

I left the glass and the bottle on the bedside table, next to a portrait of Horacio as a child.

'I promise I'll be back to see you as soon as things calm down, OK?' I got up.

'When…?'

'I don't know, a couple of weeks, when Horacio's left again.'

'He's leaving? How? Where is he going? My son… What will I do without my sweet Horacio…?'

She started sobbing again, but this time they were tired sobs, drier than streams in April. She lay back and buried her face in the pillows. I stroked her hair and left.

9.

The garden looked empty. I hurried past Horacio's window, although I couldn't see in because of the glare on the glass. Approaching the kitchen, I heard voices. I looped around the pool and stopped, leaning against the wall. In the kitchen, Panchito and Tona were in the middle of an amorous foray. He coaxed and cajoled; giggling, she insisted unconvincingly that he leave her alone. I calculated how long it would take Panchito to come round the counter if he saw me climbing the stairs. I decided to make a break for it.

'Hey, you! Where are you going? Stop or I'll shoot!' Pancho yelled. I froze on the fourth or fifth step. When I turned around, I saw his outstretched arm, forming a gun with his fingers, like in a game of cops and robbers. I darted up the stairs again. I opened the door and dashed into the empty lot, but I hadn't made it even halfway by the time Panchito knocked me onto the dusty ground. He wrenched my arms behind my back and hauled me back into the house. He tried to throw me down the stairs, but I managed to support myself against the wall, straining away from him.

'That way,' he said, jutting his chin toward the studio.

Resigned, I trudged over of my own accord. Before I could go in, though, he grabbed me by the neck so he could present me as his prey.

'Here he is, boss. Found him. He was trying to fly the coop.'

'Easy, Francis, we don't want to break him. This gentleman is my guest, you're to treat him with the respect he deserves. Go on, why don't you get the boys. Have them bring in the equipment.'

Panchito, now Francis, obeyed, looking as baffled as I felt at Horacio's defence of me. Horacio asked me to take a seat and ambled back and forth before the painting, a pot of coffee in his hand.

'Congratulations, José. You did it! This is exactly what I wanted. It's perfect. It's... a true copy!'

'Why didn't you just let me go then?'

'Oh, well, I wanted to thank you first, of course. But you're free. By all means take your leave. Francis is gone, so no one will stop you. He's not, shall we say, the sharpest knife in the drawer, so I hope you'll forgive his rash behaviour. Ah, and don't forget to stop by my office for your payment. Make it this week, because next week I'll be travelling.'

He took a sip of coffee and turned his back to me. I sensed a trick. I decided to wait for him to finish whatever he wanted to say. When he saw I wasn't getting up, he sat down across from me and rested his heels on the table.

'You do know it was only a joke, don't you? That whole business of threatening you, locking you up – just a test. A way to guarantee you'd execute the piece to perfection. You should be proud of yourself, José. You've taken a great leap forward. Now you're no mere copyist, you're a poet!'

'And your joke involved making me lose my apartment? Starving me to death? Getting your gorilla to strangle me in my sleep?'

'You're not serious? Wow, he really has it in for you, doesn't he! I never asked him to do a thing like that. As for the apartment, well, that was just a technicality. War tactics. You know you'll recover whatever you've lost a thousand times over. And you can't say it wasn't worth it, can you? Look at this… this deserves all my respect. You made it happen. There it is, *the intimate sense that shatters external form*. Don't you see?'

I turned to look at the painting, but it was as if I didn't recognise it. As if I couldn't even remember painting it.

'If it were up to me, I'd leave this *Morisca* hanging in the chapel and hand over the real thing. I'm positively blown away.'

A five-man team in white overalls appeared in the doorway to the studio, lugging all kinds of tools and devices.

'Right, let's go. We should let them do their job.' To the men, he said: 'Go right ahead, boys, here you have it. Don't forget everything we agreed on: sixteenth-century, fire-damage, the wear and tear of travel, the earthquake.'

One of the workers had a gas tank and a blowtorch. Others pulled out sanding machines, emeries and drills from their boxes. We left the studio. Behind me, I heard the roar of a flame being adjusted through the valve on the tank.

I followed Horacio towards the entrance to the vault. El Gordo was cleaning the pool and I wanted to say goodbye. I walked over and thanked him, told him I was leaving. I tried to shake his hand, but he refused. Moving away without a single glance or gesture, he continued fishing out bougainvillea blossoms, focusing intently on the long net. From a distance, he looked like a boatman guiding the house over a prim and placid ocean.

Horacio led me into the vault and we sat in exactly the same place as on that first day. As if mere hours had passed since my arrival. He took a chequebook from a drawer of the desk that doubled as his bar and began to write.

'No,' I said firmly. 'I don't want a cheque. I want you to pay me in cash.'

He looked up, surprised and scornful.

'Unless you want to find ten other copies of *La Morisca* in the art bazaar in Zapopan.'

'You're quite the negotiator, aren't you? You almost sound like me. Alright then, cash it is. I just hope you'll hold up your end of the bargain, you know. Otherwise I'll have to kill you, or at least pluck out your eyes like they did to copyists in the Middle Ages.'

'Don't worry about that. Pay me in cash and I'll forget I ever saw the painting.'

'OK, OK. But I don't have that much to hand. You'll have to come with me to the bank.'

I didn't answer, still wary of falling prey to his wiles.

'Come on then. That way I can drop you wherever you're going.'

I don't know where I found the composure, the clinical coolness that allowed me to take charge of the situation. Not a trace of fear. We got into his Alfa Romeo and drove to a bank a few streets away, on Avenida Acueducto. The executive who received us piled six packs of bills onto his desk, all wrapped in security tape.

'I understand you do not have a briefcase, sir, is that correct?' he said with a slight hint of suspicion. I replied that I didn't. 'Just a moment, please. Let me see what I can come up with.'

He returned with a green plastic bag, the kind you'd use for groceries. A branded souvenir for housewives. Horacio regarded the scene from afar, resting his cheek against his fist. He seemed entertained.

'I'm terribly sorry, but this was all I could find,' said the man, gently settling the bills into the bag as if they were fat, ripe avocados.

We left the bank and got back into Horacio's car.

'Where to?'

'López Mateos and Avenida México.'

'Staying with a relative?'

'No. Since you've left me homeless, I'll stay a couple of nights at the Quinta Real.'

'Ah, good choice. The hotelier is a client of mine. I'll tell him to offer you a discount if you like.'

'No, that won't be necessary, thanks.'

'Oh come on, José, you're making me feel bad. Like I'm some evil, abominable creature, when all I wanted was to help! You can't pretend you'll go back to painting like you used to after all this… Imagine what you'll be capable of now. You still don't realise what you've become. But you will, sooner or later, and then you'll thank me.'

He drove slowly down the sunny streets. I was silent, the bag of money perched on my lap.

'You have to understand that nothing worthwhile is ever easy. It has to be a struggle if it's going to work out. That's just the way it is. You've passed the test and now you're ready, don't you see? I wish you'd agree to keep working with me. You can't imagine how many doors it would open for you.'

'Forget it. I'll get out here and walk the rest of the way.'

I tried to open the door, but the child lock was on and I didn't know how to disable it.

'Wait, don't leave like this.' He parked the car under the shade of a tree. 'I don't want any hard feelings between us. I'd like to make amends for the harm I've done you. I understand you don't want to work with me, but at least let me help you out a little. Let's go to the club tonight.

I'll introduce you to the biggest collectors in the city, all the celebrities in town. Really powerful people.' He rubbed his thumb and index finger together as if stroking a wad of bills. 'It's up to you if you want to do business with them or not, but at least let me help you take that leap. It's no skin off my back. Besides, I'm going travelling, so it's not like you'll ever have to see me again if you don't want to. This way I'll lend you a hand and ease my conscience. What do you say?'

I kept quiet for a few moments. My hands were sweaty on the plastic bag.

'Alright. But I don't think I can tonight.'

'Why on earth not? Remember, I'll be gone next week. And today's the best day to go to the club! What could possibly be more important?'

'I have to get my pickup from the pound. It got towed the first day I went to see you.'

'Now that really was nothing to do with me, just so you know!' He barked a cynical laugh. 'Here, write down the licence plate number.'

He started the engine again, picked up his cell phone and dialled.

'Sergeant? I need you to help me retrieve a truck that got towed a couple of months back. It's urgent. Yes, I'll give you the info…'

All I had to do was tip the tow truck driver and meet my pickup at the hotel entrance, where Horacio had stopped to let me out.

'I'll see you at my place at seven on the dot. It's a black-tie event. If you can't rent a dinner jacket here, I'll lend you one,' he said by way of goodbye. I waved listlessly through the window and walked into what looked to me like the fanciest hotel on earth.

Before I checked in, I went to the bathroom in the lobby and extracted some cash from the bag I'd stuffed under my arm. I paid for my room upfront and went back out to receive the tow truck, which returned my pickup in a truly deplorable state. Covered in dust, tires punctured, the engine spent, empty of petrol, oil, water and brake fluid. It hurt even to look at it.

There was a garage across the street. I asked the tow truck driver to take it there and instructed the mechanic to fix whatever needed fixing. He promised to have it ready by five.

I returned to the hotel and went up to my room. I opened the curtains, breathed in the wax-scented air, took off my shoes and flopped down on the bed, pillows bouncing up around me. I lay like that for a while, doing nothing, staring at the patterns printed on the blades of the ceiling fan. Horacio was right: if it weren't for those hazy days in confinement, I'd still be thinking exactly the same way as before, and I'd keep painting just as I always had – or even stop altogether, more likely. Now it was crystal clear: I couldn't do anything else. I needed canvases, a peaceful space and tonnes of paint. My mind was flooded with relentless images, and the ideas behind them struggled to materialise in the light. I could see the world with a painter's gaze – or, better put, I needed that gaze to make sense of reality. At some point I turned over on my belly, hugged a pillow to my chest and fell into a deep sleep.

I woke after five, rejuvenated and full of energy, itching to get behind the wheel of my pickup once more. My heart raced at the sound of the engine gunning on the first go, the wheels screeching on the smooth floor of the garage. It was the same excitement I'd felt when I drove it out of the dealership for the first time. The feeling that I could drive to the ends of the earth. I went around the block a few times to warm up the engine, then pulled into the hotel parking lot. Glancing around to make sure no one was watching, I hid the bag of money under the seat, in a gap between the springs, out of sight even to someone crouching down to look.

I could have done anything then. I could have sat behind the steering wheel and driven without stopping until I reached a distant city full of birds, a place where I could start over, live as a vagabond, get a trailer and cram it with supplies, then wander around, painting in the town square, in an empty lot. Or not. Maybe my soul was already tethered to something that wouldn't let me stray very far. At the entrance to the hotel was a door with gold letters that said *concierge*. I knocked and an older man wearing a ridiculous top hat peered out.

'I need a dinner jacket. Can you help?'

'Of course, sir. Right this way, if you'd be so kind.'

I trailed him down the corridors of the hotel. I imagined a dove or a white rabbit springing out of his hat at any moment.

'I hope there's also a place for names and contact details in that excellent memory of yours,' said Horacio as we stepped onto the mezzanine of the University Club. Some twenty men in dinner suits and the occasional woman in an evening gown were scattered across the checkerboard ballroom floor. A round table in the centre displayed a large arrangement of fresh flowers. In a corner, a string quartet played classical music; the piece sounded familiar but I couldn't place it.

Clouds of cigarette and cigar smoke collected by the plaster cornices. Waiters in gloves and white jackets wove this way and that, offering drinks on silver platters.

'That grey-haired, balding fellow is Don Gabriel Covarrubias. We'll go over in a moment and I'll introduce you. The stuffy-looking, skinny one over there is Silvestre

Flores, he's quite an important collector. He launders money for Caro Quintero, but he won't be much good to you; he only cares about abstract art, nothing figurative.' He accepted a glass of sparkling wine from the waiter and took a long draught. 'You can't imagine how I detest this whole sham of contemporary art. It's an utter farce: some act as if they understand it, others as if they make it happen. I can't stand the vertigo, the smell of new plastic.' He grimaced and took another swig as if to cleanse his palette. 'Ah, look, come! I'll introduce you to Hilario Galguera instead.'

Horacio led me from one group to another, presenting me as the best painter he'd ever known. I felt like the belle of the ball that night. I rubbed shoulders with all kinds of people: erudite millionaires, ignorant millionaires, politicians, collectors, even a handful of diplomats who'd showed up early for the Ibero-American Summit, about which I knew nothing, but which dominated almost every conversation.

Of the ones who showed any interest, most gave me their cards and asked me to call and arrange a meeting. Others invited me to events, like the opera singer who promised to get me backstage at the Teatro Degollado; Don Gustavo Agraz, who offered me a personal tour of the clock tower at Jardines Alcalde; or Señorita De Alba, a legend in the antiques world. She was older than Methuselah and was said to have amassed objects of incalculable value. She insisted that I should join her for tea at her home on Avenida Hidalgo, any day at eleven o'clock sharp.

My jacket pocket was stuffed with cards and bits of paper. Unfortunately, Horacio got very drunk. He started to lose his cool and make rude interjections, like how all artists were frauds except for me. 'José Federico Burgos is my man!' he shouted before I could drag him toward the exit. The valet brought us the car, but Horacio couldn't even stand up. He handed me the keys and let me drive his extraordinarily expensive Alfa Romeo back to his place.

'A man needs a friend,' he slurred. 'I'd give anything to make you my friend. No, no, I'd give anything to paint like you. Even just a little. But all the money in the world couldn't make this hand paint. It's my mother's fault that… I'll never….' He nodded off.

We reached his house and I helped him down the stairs to his bedroom. I settled him onto the mattress and got ready to go. But Horacio begged me not to leave so soon, whined that he was lonely.

'OK, fine, I'll stay for a bit,' I said, and waited for him to fall asleep. The crickets were chirping raucously in the garden.

I switched on a lamp and flipped through a photo book about the Sahara that was sitting on the coffee table: caravans of camels and tents, cloth-draped women, cloth-draped men, the sun's glare, bald plains, more glare reheating centuries upon centuries of toasted sand. I leaned back and dozed off.

Still half-asleep, I heard the crowing of a cockerel. When I woke, I realised it wasn't a cockerel at all, but someone shrieking. A long, piercing wail ricocheted around the walls. Horacio shoved at the door with both hands and burst into the room, spitting a ferocious insult, something like *fucking dog* or *you worthless dog*; I can't remember exactly. He lunged at me, fists flying, his speech frenzied with tears and rage: 'She's dead! My mother's dead. You did this.'

I managed to dodge a few of his blows. Horacio wasn't particularly strong, but when I saw him grab a poker from the fireplace, I shrank back and bolted from the bedroom.

In the hall, in the open door of Isabel's bedroom,

Tona screamed and launched accusations at the top of her lungs.

'You gave it to her, you bastard!' she cried, brandishing the empty bottle in her fist. I tried to shake her off, but her tensed hands clutched at my clothes and hair. 'You gave her the poison, you gave her false hope,' she screeched into my ear. I gritted my teeth. Her powerful arm gripped my neck in a vice. The same hand that clenched the bottle also held a sheet of pale pink paper marked in pen, as if Isabel's death had been set down in a medical prescription she'd written out to talk herself into it.

I couldn't free myself from Tona's clutches, which gave Horacio his chance to strike me on the back of the head with the poker. The light dimmed and I collapsed. The last thing I remember seeing was the embroidered edge of white petticoats.

I opened my eyes repeatedly in the dark, not knowing if I was dead already or on the brink of it. Later, I was blinded by sun. When a ray of light shone right in my face, I finally came to, and I realised I was locked in the grotto that had served as Horacio's father's tomb: muddy floor, the walls of a cave, damp. The sunbeam came in through the grate I could now see from the inside; it was located a couple of metres above the ground. I couldn't move, but I was soon shivering uncontrollably, and I heard a voice deep in the recesses of my mind: *Move. If you don't move, you'll die in here.*

I started with my legs. They'd fallen asleep, though they seemed intact. My back was tight and contorted and it felt like all my bones had been rearranged. But no pain I'd ever experienced could compare with what I felt when I tried to move my right hand. It started in my fingertips and exploded at the base of my skull with a scream that pierced my throat.

I dragged myself as best I could toward the closest wall and leaned against it. I tugged off my cummerbund and fashioned a sling for my arm. Then I got to my feet, made my way to the mouth of the grotto and shouted 'Help!' several times... I waited a few moments. No answer. Suddenly I heard a hoarse voice yelling the same thing – 'Help, help!' – from some corner of the garden. It was El Gordo's macaw: it wasn't the first time it had heard such a plea. I felt a rush of terror to think that the bones of Horacio's father had to be around here somewhere. His skull – a snake slithering into one eye socket and out the other – foretold the fate of my own. I slid down to the ground again as the panic swelled, mining my nerves one by one.

I gathered my courage and decided to use the last ray of light to search for the man's remains. I groped around on the floor with my left hand until I felt something. A rag. A large, thick rag that reeked of urine. I pulled it toward the waning sunbeam and immediately recognised the checked pattern. It was Socket's blanket. Socket and his toothache. Socket and the photo of *La Morisca* I'd given him: the photo I now found pinned with chewing gum on a wall of the grotto.

The sunbeam vanished. The fever and tremors floored me again. I don't know how long I slept or how many nightmares I had, although none held a candle to the horrors of reality. The same ray of light creaked its way back into the darkness and showed me a chink in the cavern, a crack through which, I realised, Socket must somehow have fled to safety.

I tried to wriggle through, but my body was too stout to fit. I would have had to subject myself to months of a dervish's rigors before I ever got as thin as Socrates. But I was so desperate that I kept trying until I could budge neither forward or back. For a moment I thought

I'd be stuck there forever. Sandwiched in the darkness, in the depths of the house that had swallowed me whole. I was struggling to free myself when I heard, among the echoes in the crevice, the sound of choral singing. It was Isabel's wake.

That night, I quenched my thirst by drinking rivulets of rainwater that trickled down among the rocks. I regained some strength and shook off my fear. I had to find a way out. Meanwhile, my right hand had gone stiff, the flesh stuck to the sling. It throbbed on my chest as if I had two hearts: one inside me and a second resting on top, bruised and aching.

I stood on tiptoe at the mouth of the grotto to see if I could reach the key. If Horacio had left me for dead, then maybe the key was still under the mill. I needed two working hands to get up. I wouldn't have had any trouble with both, but with just one hand gripping the bars I couldn't bear my own weight long enough to pull my torso up onto the ledge. After countless attempts, all I managed to do was knock a bunch of candles and saints and fake flowers into the grotto. Then it occurred to me to stack up the glass candle holders. Using this tiny ladder, on about the thousandth attempt I finally managed to haul myself up into the entrance. Now the hard part: overturning the millstone on the right. I twisted desperately, trying to reach it with my left hand, but it was no use; the stone was too far away. I repositioned myself and tried again with the tip of my foot. At last, I rolled over the stone. All I saw was moss, dry leaves and woodlice.

Frantic, I rattled the grate, kicked the bars with what little strength I had left and growled to stifle the scream of rage brewing in my throat. I heard footsteps on the grass. Startled, I jumped back into the dark of the cave. It was El Gordo. He dropped off three oranges, a bag of nuts and the key to the grotto. I wanted to hoist myself up and thank him, ask what was going on, although of course I knew he wouldn't be able to tell me. I could only see his silent face. He glanced fearfully back towards the house and ran off again.

For the third time, a sunbeam impaled the darkness. I couldn't bear it any more: the pain in my hand, the fever. I focused on the sounds. There was a lot of commotion that morning. Voices, people going up and down the stairs. Boxes being dragged, suitcases being wheeled, heavy objects. After midday, everything went quiet. I heaved myself up to the entrance again and peered through the bars. Even the treetops were still. I fitted the key into the padlock and emerged. The house was deserted and so silent it seemed to be holding its breath in hiding.

The power had been cut. The pool was covered with leaves and flowers. I rushed into the kitchen and grabbed an overripe avocado, orphaned in the fruit bowl, and stuffed it into my mouth. Almost all the food in the refrigerator had spoiled. The tap water ran muddy and brown. It was as if months had gone by. I quelled my hunger with some tins I found in the pantry.

I wandered the house to make sure no one else was there. I looked for a first aid kit in Horacio's bathroom. The sight of my broken, rotting hand was like a sucker punch to the stomach. In a frenzy, I kicked over the bin, hurled Horacio's perfumes and lotions onto the ground, shattered the mirror with his silver brush. Once I'd calmed down a bit, I rinsed off the dried blood and wrapped my arm in a silk shirt I yanked from the closet. I rushed upstairs – I needed to get to a hospital as soon as possible. But when I reached the door, I realised in horror that it was locked. I turned around and looked down at the house from above: the high walls, the fretwork stark against the sky. A labyrinth teeming with monsters would have been less terrifying.

I tried every possible way to get out. When I saw that it was hopeless, I devoted my energy to saving my hand. I soaked it in warm salt water and bathed it in iodine, but it wouldn't do much good. The fingers were broken, the wound already rank and swollen. I went into the garden, sat on a sunbed by the pool and tried to figure out how to get out. It seemed I'd have no choice but to bite the bullet and jump.

'And that's when we found you – after you'd gone over the edge,' says the man with impish eyes. He's perched on the edge of my bed, cane hooked over one arm. 'Remember? Benito Albarrán and I were halfway through our game when you came crashing down out of the blue, right on top of the ninth hole.'

Sensing my confusion, he draws closer, mimicking my baffled look. Then he smiles gently and uncrosses his arms.

'Be strong, young man. Hang in there. Everything will be fine once you're back home, you'll see. You belong to that place and now you belong to *her* as well. But you must know that by now.' He waves his cane in the air, then taps the ground with it as though it's a sorcerer's staff. He walks off without another word.

I hear voices all around me. They rise in volume; someone is distressed, cries out for the doctor. The hospital wing hums with anxiety, with murmurs echoing round the walls. A bird alights on the cross in an alcove. I take a deep breath.

The nun approaches, accompanied by a stocky man in paint-spattered overalls. I recognise him: it's Gabriel Flores, the mural painter.

'I'm so glad you're awake! It takes a lot of courage to do what you've done, to keep going in spite of it all. I admire that. It's a pleasure to finally meet you.'

'But... we spoke the other night, in the main wing. You showed me your murals.'

'I wish that were so.' His voice is thick, calm. 'If I'd seen you, I'd have done everything in my power to keep you from wandering the halls in the state you were in, you can be certain of that. I'm told you mentioned my name in your hallucinations, but, to be honest, I'm not sure how you know me. Have we met?' I tell him we haven't. 'Ah, no matter. You probably won't remember, but it was Mother Juanita who found you on the floor that night, burning with fever. You were suffering from severe sepsis. Your hand was pinned under the weight of your body, which made things worse. The doctors worked miracles to save it. We heard that you're a painter too. I myself asked them to bear that in mind. And look – it seems to be much better now.'

I glance at the hand beside me, as though surprised it's still there. I try writing in the air with my left hand to see if it's true – that the abilities of one hand can be transferred to the other – but no, the left remains as clumsy as ever.

'So tell me, José, what did you say to me that night, or dream you said to me?'

It would be many weeks, many agonising procedures and several surgeries, before the orthopaedist decided to discharge me for further rehabilitation with a physiotherapist. He warned me it would be a long and arduous process before I regained full mobility in my hand, but I would definitely be able to paint again. He made me promise to invite him to my first exhibition: 'And it had better be good, you hear, or I'll have your hand right back the way it was,' he joked as he signed my release form and wrote out my prescriptions.

Don Gabriel said he'd come by early to say goodbye. It's eleven o'clock. I put on the clothes Mother Juanita collected for me. I don't know what I'll do once I'm back out on the street. I guess I'll start by trying to find my pickup. I'd parked it in front of Horacio's house, although I can't imagine it's still there. I take the set of keys with the snake keychain from the bureau and put them in my pocket. Mother Juanita gives me a hug and I thank her repeatedly for her kindness. She blesses me with the sign of the cross. I ask her to say goodbye to the other nuns who looked after me.

I find Don Gabriel in the central wing. He talks like a loving father as his son embarks on a long journey.

'Take good care of yourself, José. And take care of that hand, so you can get back to painting just like you did before.'

'Don't worry, that's what my other hand is for,' I reply, alluding to the dream he's heard all about by now. We laugh. He hugs me and asks for the millionth time if I need help with anything: lodging, transportation. I insist that I don't. He knows I want to figure things out myself and lets me go.

I head for the exit. Before I descend the very first step, I see it in the distance. *Is it… It is! It has to be…* I cross the street and move closer. There, in the shade of an orange tree, is my pickup, parked and waiting for me like a trusty steed. I can't believe it. It must have been El Gordo; who else? How did he know I was here, in this hospital? When did he drive it over? How and where can I track him down to thank him? I haven't the faintest idea. I dig into my pocket for the keys that have miraculously accompanied me all this time, and unlock the door. It smells of sun-steeped upholstery, pine oil, disinfectant spray. I laugh. If only I had someone to share this laughter with. I laugh harder when I peer under the seat and grope around until I feel the green plastic bag with the money inside, hot as bread.

I'm trembling. My hands shake as I try to grip the keys and start the engine. Where to go? Where to start over? San Miguel de Allende, Oaxaca, Mexico City? No man has ever been so free.

Luckless Lalo's shop is a few blocks from the hospital. I head there first, ducking under a half-closed metal curtain. I hear the clicking of domino tiles in the back room. The grimy cat leaps onto the desk and strains to sniff my bandage.

'What's up, man? Long time no see! What happened to you this time?'

'Saw accident. Nothing serious.'

'Have a seat. How about a drink?'

'Thanks, but I'm just passing through. I came to drop off a piece, if you'd like it.'

'On consignment? Because I'm stone broke right now, you know.'

'No, don't worry. Whatever you can milk it for. It's in rough shape.'

'Let's see it, then. Never look a gift horse in the mouth.'

We went to unload Señora Chang's triptych. The sun had corroded the paint and the dry glaze had peeled. There was no use returning it to her and trying to explain what she'd never understand.

'Hey, what happened with that job I sorted for you a while ago? How'd it turn out?'

'Just fine, Lalo. Over and done with. It was an easy gig, a restoration.'

'Ah, that's good. Because I heard the guy was up to something shady. Dealing drugs in lord knows what country. A real mess.'

'Is that right?' I feigned indifference.

'Yeah, sounds like things got ugly. It was just a couple of weeks ago. That's why I was worried. I said to myself,

Let's hope José didn't get tangled up in all that.'

'Nah, Lalo, nothing like that. Here I am, no drama –
just nose to the grindstone, same as ever.'

'Good, good. Well, I'll see if I can find a buyer for this.
Are you off somewhere?'

'No, why?'

'I don't know. Just wondering. You looked like you
might be heading somewhere far away.'

'No, I'm around. I'll be back before you know it to
nag you about my paintings.'

'Anytime. Come visit whenever you like and we'll
have a tequila or two. Oh, and we've got to celebrate!
Malinche's going to be a mother, did you hear?'

'I hadn't, but that's great news. I'm glad you told me,
I'll get in touch to congratulate her.'

I get back into my truck and take Revolución to
González Gallo. At Lázaro Cárdenas, the avenue becomes
the highway, and the more highway there is, the safer I'll
feel hitting the accelerator.

As I pass the Zapotlanejo bridge, the squeak of a seat
makes me turn around. The man with impish eyes is
sitting behind me. He's holding his cane between his legs
with both hands.

'The canyon's awfully pretty, isn't it? You don't even
expect it, and suddenly it's right there. Out of nowhere,
and green, so green...'

I act as if I haven't heard him. I stare at the road.

'Haven't you heard of the curse of the Huentitán
Canyon? Because of the Caxcan Indians, who hurled
themselves into the abyss to escape the shackles of the
conquering Spaniards. That's why nothing prospers there,
even in a place as beautiful as this. Haven't you noticed?
The whole city turns its back on it. Only poor people
live there. The gringos can only dream of a view like
this – the earth spreading out before them. Now tell

me, when was the last time you stopped at the Cola de Caballo lookout?'

'Who are you, anyway?' I say at last, since he won't stop talking. 'A hallucination, a poltergeist, or what?'

'My name is Luis Barragán. And I'm with you right now because you're heading in the wrong direction. The house is that way.' He jerks a thumb over his shoulder.

I pull over and stop the truck in a clearing by the side of the highway. The manoeuvre requires my full attention, and when I look back at him, he's gone. I get out of the vehicle, take a deep breath, try to calm down. I take a few steps toward the slope and duck behind some bushes to empty my bladder. I look up at the dreary sky. Clusters of costmary sway like yellow waves, flooding the scene with the fragrance of herb stalls in the Corona market. It's not losing my mind that troubles me. What troubles me is the strength of the bond, the blind knot that tugs at me from deep inside – the harder I pull the more it hurts.

I get back into the pickup and start the engine. I glance both ways across the highway and rev into motion with a 180-degree swerve that makes the asphalt crunch. I accelerate. I don't want to think. All I can think is that I don't want to think, and I keep picturing the Caxcans plunging off the cliff, their faces lit with wonder at themselves.

I drive back into the city, travelling the streets I know so well, and park by the entrance with the snub-nosed lions. I slip my fingers under the metal door and tug on the wire to open it. I cross the empty lot. I open the shattered glass door and recognise the cool air, the scent of the garden. The house receives me with the euphoric shout of a man running naked down the grassy slope, leaping off the edge of the pool and landing with a great liquid explosion that fills the air with life. I see the snarl of grey hair floating over the navy blue. Socrates swims on his back with his eyes closed. I reach the terrace, where the macaw is shuffling back and forth across the back of a chair. He retracts his feathers at the sight of me and releases a drop of excrement, utterly unabashed.

El Gordo emerges from the house, looking anxious, and stops in front of me. Without meeting my eyes, he takes my left hand and shakes it. I feel his childish touch, the damp little pillow of his thumb. I pull him close and give him a hug. I'd like it to be a proper bear hug, but his body stiffens and he hops cheerfully away. He offers the macaw his arm to roost on and raises a blackberry to its beak.

Socrates gets out of the pool and ties a towel around his waist. His almond eyes flash through his wet mane.

'I went to see the dentistry students and they pulled my tooth out, see?' He pulls a flap of cheek to show me the hole in his gum. 'Didn't hurt a bit.'

Still bewildered, I don't know what to say.

'I'm glad you're here,' he adds. 'I can't eat all this chicken by myself.'

There's a large box of Kentucky Fried Chicken on the kitchen counter. He picks up a piece and takes a bite. He runs back to the pool, pulls off his towel and throws himself back into the water, food still in hand.

I laugh. The laughter tickles me from inside, bubbling up and streaming from my eyes in cool, sweet tears. I go into the house. I walk down the hallway to the very back as if someone there were calling my name. I take off my shoes before stepping out into the courtyard with the clay jugs, so I can feel the damp soil under my feet. The sliding door is ajar and the curtain billows, but there's no one on the other side. Swollen with blossoms, the jacaranda tree rains into the courtyard with every gust. A sparrow trills its momentary hymn and flies off. It's the beginning.

CHARCO PRESS

Director & Editor: Carolina Orloff
Director: Samuel McDowell

www.charcopress.com

The Forgery was published on
80gsm Munken Premium Cream paper.

The text was designed using Bembo 11.5 and ITC Galliard.

Printed in March 2022 by TJ Books
Padstow, Cornwall, PL28 8RW using responsibly
sourced paper and environmentally-friendly adhesive.